Why Paul Ferroll Killed His Wife by Caroline Clive

Caroline Meysey-Wigley was born on June 24th 1801 in Brompton Grove, London, the daughter of Edmund Meysey-Wigley, Esq., of Shakenhurst, Worcestershire, M.P. for Worcester, and his wife, Anna Maria Meysey.

A severe illness contracted when she was three left her with several after-effects chief amongst them was lameness.

During her lifetime she became a respected and well-regarded poet and author. All of her works were published anonymously, using the pen name, "V".

In 1840, her 'IX Poems' appeared in a small duodecimo, which Hartley Coleridge reviewed in the September edition of the Quarterly Review:—

"We suppose V stands for Victoria, and really she queens it among our fair friends. Perhaps V will think it a questionable compliment, if we say, like the late Baron Graham to Lady —, in the Assize Court at Exeter, 'We beg your ladyship's pardon, but we took you for a man.' Indeed, these few pages are distinguished by a sad Lucretian tone, such as very seldom comes from a woman's lyre. But V is a woman, and no ordinary woman certainly; though, whether spinster, wife, or widow, we have not been informed. The stanzas printed by us are, in our judgment, worthy of any one of our greatest poets in his happiest moments."

It was very fine praise indeed and was only one of many.

Later that year on November 10th, she married the Reverend Archer Clive. The union would produce a son (1842) and a daughter (1843).

Caroline continued to write and the following year, 1841, published a second edition of 'IX Poems' which was followed by 'I Watched the Heavens' (1842); 'The Queen's Ball' (1847); 'Valley of the Rea' (1851); and 'The Morlas' (1853). She now also began to add novels to her publications beginning with one from the popular sensational genre: 'Paul Ferroll: A Tale' (1855). It was hugely successful.

In literary terms, aside from her poems, her reputation is most burnished by 'Paul Ferroll' and its sequel, 'Why Paul Ferroll Killed his Wife'. The first is generally accepted to be the most superior of all her works and passed into several editions and translations. It was only with the fourth edition that the concluding chapter, which brought the story down to the death of Paul Ferroll, was added. 'V' was now a respected and popular novelist to go with her glowing reputation as a poet.

'Paul Ferroll' is considered the precursor of the genre 'sensational novel' or of what may be called the novel mystery. Caroline was included in the forefront of the sensational novelists of the 19th-century, anticipating the works of Wilkie Collins, Charles Reade, Miss Braddon, and many others, writing of human nature as defined by its energies, neither diagnosing it like a physician, nor analysing it like a priest.

Caroline's health was always a delicate issue and for many years prior to her death she was a confirmed invalid.

Caroline Clive died when her dress caught fire whilst she was seated in her boudoir and among her papers on July 13th 1873, at Whitfield, Herefordshire.

Index of Contents

WHY PAUL FERROLL KILLED HIS WIFE

CHAPTER I

A long gallery opening on each side to small rooms gave the inhabitants of St. Cécile's Monastery access both to them and to the larger apartment which was inhabited by the Reverend Mother herself. This latter room was of an oblong shape, very bare of furniture, and of all kinds of decoration. The windows were without curtains; there was but one table, and on it stood a crucifix. Two benches by the wall were all the accommodation for sitting down. The one figure which occupied the chamber required not even so much, for she was kneeling in the middle of the floor, with support of no kind, and quite upright, except her head, which was bowed under the thick cloth or veil hanging over it, and which concealed even her hands.

"She is praying," said a nun, looking into the room, "you had better wait;" and these words she addressed to a young girl who accompanied her, in the ordinary tone of conversation, such as befitted the occupations of the place.

The young girl advanced into the room, and herself went down on her knees at a little distance from the Superior, running over her beads while she waited till she might speak. She was very simply dressed in white, with parted hair, like a child, but abundant and beautiful, falling low on low shoulders and delicately rounded waist. Her face was fair, with very little colour, and the eyes, which she raised often, while she slid her beads through her fingers, had a simplicity of religious expression, such as fades even in those happy enough once to possess it, when the habits of a pious childhood come to be contradicted by those of the general world.

When the Superior rose from her knees, so did Elinor, and advanced towards the elder lady, who kissed her on the forehead, and gave a blessing. The conversation was in French, though the girl was English, for it was in a Convent of Brittany that the scene took place. It did not begin in the tone supposed to be exclusively that of Lady Abbesses.

"Has Louisa finished the marking of all your shifts, my dear? Are they ready?"

"Yes, dear Mother, and packed up," said Elinor.

"And have you heard whether Madame Néotte is come."

"Yes, that is what I came here to tell you, as you desired."

"Then to-morrow you leave us," said the Superior, in a melancholy voice.

"It is you who have determined it," said Elinor.

"Ah, my child! your guardian believes it best; it is his doing."

"And I shall come back," said the girl.

"No, dear, you will never do that. I know your feelings better than you do. It will be a hard parting with us all, but when you are away you will be glad. You will enjoy the world, you will choose it, and you will be welcome in it. No; you will never wish to come back here. I have known many gentle girls like you, who could not find what they wanted here. They require to be carried along—not to walk alone, as in a convent."

"Am I one of those," said Elinor, catching hold of the Abbess's hand and passionately kissing it; "I who have been so happy?"

"And have made us all happy—but you must go. Sit down a little while, let us talk for the last time. The world is full of snares, my dear."

"What are they?" said Elinor. "What will they tempt me to do?"

"Vanity, the pride of life, the lusts of the devil," answered the Superior. "You must be prepared for all. Some will pretend that you have beauty; some will praise your voice, as if you were a musician; some will talk to you of the world—and all, all for their own bad ends."

"What are those ends?" asked Elinor, again.

The Abbess, was a little puzzled. "Man," said she, solemnly, "is a creature going about to devour. Listen not to him, go not near him, keep him far from you. He will hurt you, he will destroy you; you have already learned this; now is your time to practise. Keep your eyes from his face, keep your speech from his commerce. One day it may come to pass that your guardian may select one who is to be your husband. Then submit yourself to the will of your superiors, and adopt the state of life which shall be allotted you; but till such a fate is brought to your door, remember that a maiden must keep her finger on her lips and her heart full of thoughts holy and virtuous, avoiding the very shadow of sin."

Elinor was set thinking what these sins could be; but she resolved, at all events, to do right, and to keep the precepts of her early friend in her memory.

She continued talking with the Reverend Mother as long as convent duties permitted; then, for the last time, partook the Evening Service and assisted to make the vesper beautiful by her exquisite voice, against the world's estimation of which the Superior thought she had successfully warned her.

She rose that night for Vigils; and next morning was up at Matins—the last time of doing these duties making them seem to her as if she would fain never cease to do them; and when the hour for her journey arrived, the wrench of the first roots she had ever struck in hearts and places, overwhelmed her with a girlish sorrow, which, fortunately, was not put to such proof as an offer to remove it would have been; for there is no saying how her wish to remain in the Convent would have been modified, if the chaise into which she so sobbingly stepped had been ordered back into its old remise.

CHAPTER II

On the English side of the Channel, which our heroine was about to cross, a different scene was passing in the early life of one of the opposite sex.

A young man, four years older than Elinor (who was just seventeen), had passed that summer a triumphant Examination at Oxford, and heaped on himself every honour which it was possible for its young members to obtain. He had been accustomed to success ever since he became a school-boy; and he was so far from satiated by it, that he already looked upon all his achievements as mere marks of past progress, and on himself as now about to begin the career which contained objects really worthy of his ambition.

He was an orphan, never acquainted with father or mother; wholly unconscious of tender influences on his boyhood, and of domestic sympathy with his successes and desires. He had come not to want them; disappointment he had not had, and the hard measure of public applause suited him better than the fond exaggerations of home, to which he had not grown up, nor been bettered by them. Life was a fine, hard reality to him; he knew it, for evil and good, and while he destroyed every illusion as fast as they courted him, he looked keenly to its enjoyments and rated them by the vast power of pleasure within him which he shared with most healthy and active human beings.

He was passing some weeks at a country house, where his late very hard work gave zest to the summer repose in which the old place lay buried. Long, solitary, morning walks in the heavenly beauty of a hot July did his thinking faculties good, after their late stretch upon other men's thoughts. The society of well educated women, their music, their vivacity, their fancies; the riding parties, the evenings when there was dancing, or the garden by moonlight, and the pleasure of pretending to feelings, and, as it were, acting them, for they were no better to him than a play, these things suited him for a little while, till the moment should come for executing the projects in his head which would drive all the present scene far away.

He had everything to recommend him to the world. A fine person, full of health and strength, a fortune and a place which were competent to ordinary wishes, and had been augmented by all the savings of a well managed minority; a high reputation for ability; and natural claims on certain great names for assistance in entering on his career. His manner was more taking than winning, he took hold on society as if it were his due place, and his admirable tact made him hold it gracefully, and to the delight of his companions.

These qualities and advantages had made a strong impression on the fancy of the young lady who presided over the house. She was the owner's sister, a few years older than my hero (whom I will call Leslie, though I do not assert that such was indeed his name); she was handsome, rich, and hitherto courted by all whom she had a mind should do so. But it was not so with her present guest; he often seemed on the brink of fascination, and then, like Sampson, burst the withies like burnt flax and was as free as ever. The irritation of this state of things was excessive; she longed to break through the feminine restraints which bound her, and ask him if indeed he cared for her or not. The absolute impossibility of thus setting herself free was a galling chain, for ever working on the wounded place; and the necessity of a smiling face, and disengaged manner, at times when she was fretting at her heart's core, acquainted her with a torment which the daughters of Eve sometimes heavily endure.

"Let us ride this afternoon," she said, one hot but cloudy day; "the air of the house burns one."

"With all my heart," said Leslie; "but we shall have a storm."

"I am not afraid," said Laura.

"Would I were quite sure that, in fact, you have no fears!"

"Oh! I would tell them. I am very frank, I hate concealment. It is very hard on women that they are required to be liars and deceivers."

"But that's not the case," said Leslie, "what is so delightful to a man as a frank, open nature which prints its thoughts as fast as they come into the mind."

"So you say, but you know it is not so—at least, not unless a woman has no thought whatever, except the price of a dress or the hope of a ball."

"Oh, that would not pay the expense of printing or reading either," said Leslie; "but what has this to do with your first plan of riding? Shall we go?"

"Yes; Mrs. Axross, you will ride? and Captain Bertham—ring; the horses are ready in case we should want them. Come and put on your habit."

When they got on horseback, Leslie perversely kept with Mrs. Axross, a timid horsewoman, and in consequence of being occupied with genuine fear, a rather dull companion. They fell behind the others, whose horses stepped out freely under lightly held bits, nor did Miss Chanson know how to alter the order of their progress. When she contrived, under pretence of pointing out a view, or a remarkable tree, to get back to the loiterers, she still found that Leslie adhered to his first companion, and suffered her again to get before him.

"How I hate a horse that can't walk," she said, at last, impatiently striking her own, which bounded at the unjust assault and tossed his head angrily.

"Well, then let us gallop," said Leslie, laughing, for he read her heart exactly. "My companion," he added, as they went off, "thinks only of keeping her seat. When she gets home safe, she will have fulfilled the sole purpose of riding out."

"Well, I'm better than that," said Laura, her spirits rising instantly, "I can enjoy all when there is anything to enjoy—but Captain Bertham is so stupid."

Leslie laughed again, for he knew that Captain Bertham did not deserve a reproach of which he felt himself to be the indirect cause.

"How can anyone be dull with you for a companion," said he, again, as they increased their pace and went gaily along. Laura was pleased, she did not consider that she had provoked the compliment, and that it is only voluntary attentions from a man that tell.

"Here come the great raindrops," said Leslie, as the first of the storm fell one by one.

"Oh, no! it is only the last of a shower. See, it is blowing over."

"I don't see it at all, but if you order me to see it, I will."

"I do, then," said Laura, gaily; "so let us go on."

"Was that lightning or not?" said Leslie, as a flash startled their horses, and thunder rolled at a distance.

"It was not," said Laura; "come on."

"On, on, to the end of the world under your guidance."

But now the rain at once arrived and poured upon them.

"What will Mrs. Axross do," said Laura, laughing; "she will walk her horse all the way home, for fear he should jump at the storm. We must turn back and look for them."

Leslie rather wondered she should do so, instead of profiting by her present tête-à-tête with him; but presently he understood the manœuvre. When they came to a cross road, she examined the footmarks on the road, and declared it was most extraordinary, but certainly their companions had gone the wrong way.

"They will get lost in the wood," she said; "and what will Mr. Axross say, if we go home without his wife? Let us canter up here and set them right. We shall overtake them in a minute."

"You will be wet through," said Leslie. "No, no, canter home!"

"I don't care; go home if you like."

"No, I am yours, to the very skin" said Leslie, venturing on a brutality.

Miss Chanson did not look angry, and on they went, away from home. Presently a little farmhouse appeared in sight.

"They have taken shelter there," said the lady, "no doubt. Come, let us see if they are to be found;" and arriving at the door, she jumped from her horse, saying to the farmer, who came out at the sound of horses, "My friends are here, are not they? Come, Mr. Leslie."

He followed, after first putting the horses into the stable, and giving them over to the care of the farmer's boy, and found, his companion standing before the kitchen fire, her hat off, her hair let down to dry, and her habit open.

"The weather is too bad to stay in, is not it?" she said, as he came in. "Let us wait till the storm goes by;" and she pulled her dress together.

"A lucky storm for me," said Leslie, glancing at her disarranged toilette. "Why are these lovely tresses locked up in ribbon and garlands—not always thus delightfully visible?"

Laura affected embarrassment, and hastily twisted them in her hands, but yielded to slight impulse from Leslie to release them. Finally she placed herself in a very picturesque attitude on what is called the settle, by the fire, and Leslie carried on briskly the conversation she affected.

"All this time," said he, at last, when the flirtation became a little wearisome, "what is become of Mrs. Axross?"

"I had almost forgotten her," said Laura, softly, with a smothered sigh.

"I had quite done so," said Leslie, sighing also.

"Only you recollected her," said Laura, a little reproachfully.

"Nay, the storm is over. It is getting late. I would not have you catch cold for the world—I would not be responsible for the anxiety your absence will create—I would not have you exposed to further rain—I would ......"

"Get home in time for dinner," interrupted Laura, very impatiently. Then checking herself, she added, as gaily as she could, "which would be an excellent thing, for I am very hungry."

"Then heaven forbid you should wait!" said Leslie. "I'll fetch the horses in a moment."

Accordingly he went himself to the stable, and forgot to lament the loss of the beautiful curls, which were twisted under the hat when he came back; and placing Laura on her horse, they rode home together, the lady feeling in herself that hollowness in her satisfaction which comes when the foundation of a very gay and promising structure wants perfect solidity.

"How very handsome he is," she said to herself, as she ran up the house-steps; "how agreeable—and I don't feel sure he will make himself agreeable next time—that makes one curious to be with him again."

The butler stopped her in the hall, and said, "Miss Elinor Ladylift was arrived."

"Ha! our little nun," said she, turning back to Mr. Leslie; "we did not expect her till to-morrow. Come and see her."

He followed her into the room, and saw standing by the table a young figure, perfectly enveloped in a gray cloak, while a veil concealed her features from any one at a little distance. The only characteristic which he could observe was, that the flowers on the table trembled, as if the hand which rested on it gave them that motion.

"Oh! my dear, I did not know you would be here to-day. I beg your pardon for not being here to receive you. You forgive me, don't you?"

"Yes!" said a low, timid voice.

Miss Chanson laughed. "That's all right! Then come along with me, for I am wet through: you would not have me die of cold, would you?"

"No!" said the voice.

"Right, again! I'll show you your room —but first I'll present Mr. Leslie to you. This is Mr. Leslie, my dear."

"Is it?" said the voice again.

"Yes, indeed!" and again Laura laughed, looking up at the young man sportively, and taking the girl's arm went out of the room with her. "There's no fear that she will captivate any one whom I choose for myself, especially such a man as that, so brilliant himself, and so fond of intellect and manner," thought she.

That perfect security at first sight generally ends in a total contradiction. I have remarked it as often as the case of security has taken place.

"She is tired and frightened, and won't come to dinner," said Miss Chanson, as she entered the drawing-room after dressing. "No wonder! the inside of a convent is all she knows of life."

"What does she look like?" asked her brother, a man five-and-twenty years older than the bright Laura, and an indifferent, idle bachelor, who disregarded his appearance, and looked yet ten years older than he was, in consequence.

"She is a pale, slight girl," said Laura, "and expects to be devoured by all of us. She has the least possible French accent, and moves about like a mouse."

CHAPTER III

The next day, Elinor appeared at breakfast, coming into the room close at the side of her hostess, to whom she clung, and sat down in the next chair, which vexed Laura, for it was Mr. Leslie's habitual place. He took the one below Elinor, and endeavoured to engage her in conversation, but was received like an enemy, and did not seek to avoid Miss Chanson's looks of intelligence, who remarked silently on the repulses he suffered.

The impression on him, however, was not exactly what he allowed Laura to believe. He remarked the delicate shape of the pale face, the ease of the slight figure, the fine form of the hands, which, if not very white as yet, were formed in the noblest feminine model. Her gray gown was perfectly simple, and it was quite uninteresting to him whether it was cut fashionably or unfashionably. The eyes, which were kept cast down on her plate so pertinaciously, excited his curiosity; he wanted to find some phrase which should raise them, that he might see them. Interest was awakened, but do and say what he would, he never succeeded, during all that breakfast, in making her look at him. She disappeared when it was over, and he saw her not again till after dinner, when, on coming into the drawing-room, he found her seated close to Miss Chanson, diligently at work. The latter was becoming a little tired of such close companionship; she could not rise from her chair, but what Elinor did the same, thereby preventing many manœuvres hitherto easy to practise.

"My dear child, if you like that place, keep it," said she; "the lamp suits your work, and I must go to talk to that stupid old lady, whom it is my duty to amuse."

"Shall I go," said Elinor. "They always used to send me to talk to Madame Les Forces."

"Did you succeed?" said Laura, laughing sarcastically.

"Yes, sometimes."

"But you don't know this lady—shall you have the courage?"

"Why not?"

"Nay, you will not speak one syllable to Mr. Leslie."

"No!"

"And why?" said Laura. "I talk to him—we all talk."

"The Reverend Mother said I must not."

"Did she say you might speak to none but women?" said Leslie, very gently.

"Yes!"

"Oh! that's excellent!" cried Laura. "My dear nun, you must get rid of some of those maxims; you are in a very different place from your nunnery. Don't make yourself ridiculous."

The young girl coloured excessively; she was too young to bear being ridiculous, too, fond of her habitual teachers to fancy they could be misinformed. She was perplexed, and rising, shrank away to the stupid lady, whose work she began admiring; and as long as no one else heard her voice, contrived to keep up a dialogue.

"What a quaint little creature!" said Miss Chanson, "But now I'll do my part to amuse the other stupid people, by giving you all some music."

"Do," said Mr. Leslie; "though you know I am so lost in dulness as to talk most when music is best."

"I know that; but at all events I entertain you even in that case."

She said this rather sentimentally; and Mr. Leslie opened the piano-forte, and talked a little nonsense while she arranged her books. When fairly embarked, and when other people collected round her, and they were all interested with her performance and their own, he drew gradually to the side of Elinor, and watched his chance of speaking to her. She listened to the music, which was very good, with great interest; but she drew away from him, and he could do no better than some dialogue with the stupid old lady.

At last, when there was a pause in the performance, he took up his courage, and said boldly to Elinor, "You perceive, Miss Ladylift, that they are all tired, and can play and sing no more. You ought to assist them—you ought to help in amusing us all."

She rose in a moment, as if bound to obey whoever commanded her, and walked towards the piano-forte.

"Mr. Leslie told me I ought to sing," she said. "Ought I?"

"To be sure, if you can. But what—not psalm tunes?"

"Very well, I will not. I know a great many airs which Frère du Lap taught all the pensionnaires."

"I should like to hear Frère du Lap's scholar very much," said Laura.

"Should you?" said Elinor, looking up at her, unconscious of the sarcasm; and she placed herself before the piano-forte.

Now nature had made her a present of a voice, such as she gives very rarely:

"It were the bul-bul, but his throat,
Tho' sweet, ne'er uttered such a note."

It was no merit of Elinor's; there seemed no object in bestowing it upon her; but she was lucky in being the one to get it, for its effect was to dispose the hearers to love her. It was as pure as the song of the angels heard by Handel, and set down by him as sung to the Shepherds; it had been well taught, also, so that it was a delight to the ear, a charm to the heart. Leslie, who was moving away, stopped as she began to sing, and turned to fasten his eyes upon her, as upon a new sense of delight, a pleasure revealed for the first time. She rose up when it was done; indeed, she had not actually sat down, but had bent one knee towards the level of the piano-forte, and played an accompaniment varying with the words. She was plainly a perfect mistress of her art; and, according to the fashion of drawing-rooms, her performance was greeted with clapping of hands, and a few bravas. She looked round, astonished; and if any one had desired another song, would have obeyed; but Miss Chanson came up with the last notes, and after a brief thank you, led her away, saying her voice seemed a little tired. She then organized other amusements, and the music was over for the evening.

Mr. Leslie contrived to elude them all, and very quietly coming up beside Elinor, he said to her,

"That song is one I shall never forget. I shall hear many more, I hope, but the first time one listens to a perfect thing it is remembered for ever."

Elinor shook her head. "My Mother told me you would say so."

"That I should say so? How could the Holy Mother know anything of me?"

"Not of you, but of all."

"She could, only say that all of us should be aware you have one of the finest voices in the world."

"Yes, she did say so—that you would try to persuade me of it."

"I don't wish it to be thought of me that I would persuade any one to believe an untrue thing. Let us consider for a moment," and he sat down beside her at the table, leaning upon it, and trying to look in her face, which was bent over her work. "You have heard the music of this evening?"

"Yes!"

"It was very good, was it not?"

"Very good, very strong; I never heard such before."

"But was there any voice as expressive as yours?"

"No!"

"Or that was so unlike a flute, or an organ, or a harp, but was so purely human; the perfection of human."

"I cannot hear my own voice."

"Surely, Miss Ladylift, you can."

Elinor knew she could, and he put the question plainly. She suddenly lifted up her large eyes upon him, and looked full into his for a moment—there was an anxiety to penetrate his meaning, but it yielded in another instant to the dread of encountering a stranger's gaze; however, he had seen those large eyes.

"You can if you will," said he; "everybody can judge themselves as well as they can judge other people, if they will be honest to themselves. And it is not being honest, to think worse of oneself than is the truth."

"My dear Mother told me my voice was such a voice as hundreds of others have."

"But what do you think yourself?"

"I believe her," said Elinor.

"Yes, surely," answered Leslie, afraid of alarming his companion. "She spoke her entire conviction, no doubt; still she judged from her Convent alone. There, perhaps, where all is holy, all dedicated to divine things, the inhabitants may be blessed, many of them, with gifts like the one you have in your voice; but it is not so in the world. You are in the world now; you must judge by what you see and hear; you may find there are things unlike those which the Reverend Mother knows."

"Oh! she cannot be mistaken," said Elinor.

"Only ask yourself whether she is," said Leslie. "If so, some things which were good guides in the convent, may lead wrong here."

Elinor answered nothing. The first doubt of the kind was painful, the more so because her honest nature saw that perhaps it was true.

After a pause, she said, "Who can I trust, then?"

"I know this outer world," said Leslie.

"But I do not know you," said Elinor; "I know nobody. I will do my best; you must not try to prevent me. If you liked my singing, I am glad of that; but perhaps you do not understand music, and then you cannot judge."

"No, perhaps I do not," said Leslie; "you know I can only say what I honestly feel."

"Yes, to be sure! I know you do that. Everybody does that," said Elinor, speaking as she had been unconsciously taught, and as she felt, that though there were wicked people in the world, nobody with whom one associates could be in the number of those wicked.

Mr. Leslie abhorred Laura for coming up and interrupting the conversation. She said she was sorry to see Elinor look so pale; no doubt she was used to very early hours in the Convent, and she had better go to bed. She did not say she thought her young friend tired; for knowing her not to be tired, she felt that Elinor would say No.

"You have persuaded the nun to talk, Mr. Leslie," said she; "how clever you are."

"It gives one an interest in succeeding, when the task is so difficult," said Mr. Leslie.

"No doubt; a woman who has the audacity to know or feel anything, and to say it, must expect the contempt of the nobler sex."

"Why so?" said Leslie, coolly.

"Men are so short-sighted, so easily taken in. If women affect simplicity and reserve, men see no further than just what those women give themselves the trouble to put on."

"Is that little girl a dissembler?"

"Oh! I suppose you can judge."

"I should judge not; but you know best."

"If I knew anything, I would not say it against my friend," said Laura. "My nature is more constant than that."

"More generous than that," said Leslie; "constant is not the word, for your acquaintance is so short. It is indeed very generous."

Laura liked the words, and did not understand further, and though she was not satisfied, she went away fancying she was.

Next morning, every one else being occupied in their rooms with what letter-writing or other business they might have, Laura, who could not lose any chance of being with Leslie, and Leslie, who could lose none of being with Elinor, and Elinor, who fixed herself upon Laura as her best safety in the new scenes, were all three in the library, standing about, looking at a print or a flower, and not knowing very well what to do. Elinor only was at ease, knitting gloves, move where she would.

"Suppose," said Leslie, "we show the wood-walk to Miss Ladylift. Would it not be a good employment of this delightful morning?"

Laura assented; that WE sounded so pleasantly to her.

Accordingly, each lady took up a parasol in the hall, and they all stepped into the perfumed air, and proceeded down some broad steps, which led from the garden to the steep wooded banks below the house. Elinor was delighted: the space, the depth below, the vast summer hall made by the wood, and the pavement of ferns, flowers, and briar, over which the shadows of the leaves scattered their moving patterns; the silence which seemed to come from far, and go afar, charmed her opening imagination. As they proceeded, a vague feeling of fear mingled with her pleasure. She had never known the sense of distance before.

"Shall we know how to go back," said she; "but no doubt you will."

"No fear of that," said Laura, looking behind at the walk they had come along; "the way is not difficult."

"And may you go here as far as you like?" said Elinor, thinking of her Convent restrictions.

"Who can doubt that?" said Laura, scornfully; "or that you may do so likewise? In a Convent they are children all their lives; but you must take off your leading-strings."

Elinor, till now, had never ceased to lean on some one for every action of her life. Yet she got a lesson then which went straight home, not to betray her want of help to those who could scoff her for it.

Leslie thought that the sooner she learned to doubt her former teachers the better. He had an idea he could give her lessons himself. They went on, therefore, on and on till Elinor, who had never known what it was to take a walk, was tired. She longed intensely for rest; her limbs ached; they required absolutely the new stringing of repose respose . Leslie observed it, and proposed to sit down, but Laura poured forth her playful scorn upon a girl who pretended not to be up to a mile-and-a-half walk. As for herself, she must confess to strength—half-a-dozen miles were nothing to her. Elinor felt ashamed; but was unconscious that Laura meant to insinuate that the fatigue was affected.

"I wish I could do like you," she said; "but I have not learned to walk."

"Dear baby," said Laura; "still at nurse? I wish I could carry you!"

Elinor looked at each companion, with the mournful simplicity of a child who has committed a fault it does not comprehend. Leslie was enchanted.

"It is a science you must practise," said he. "It was a fault not to have attended to your education in that respect."

Elinor was quite ready to acknowledge herself wrong, and to feel inwardly that her bringing up was not so faultless as she had thought.

At this moment, however, her wishes were all limited to rest, and gladly did she sink upon the seat at which Leslie prevailed on Laura to stop; but Laura was so restless, that Leslie at last started up with a new project in his head, and proposed that they two alone should make for the point at which Laura had intended to reach, and should leave their companion to enjoy a little repose before they returned for her to go home.

"Unless you are afraid," said Laura, turning round on Elinor.

"No, I am not afraid, for you say there is no danger," said Elinor.

And now Leslie hurried his companion away, and pushing himself into the highest spirits, rallied her on her activity, her delightful health and strength, till Laura, quite deceived, quickened her pace to the very utmost, and went over hill and dale at his side, with no idea but that of keeping up the contrast between herself and the timid Elinor.

It was not till he had carried her along with him to a point much nearer to the house than to Elinor, that he suddenly affected to remember their charge.

"Meantime, what have we done with your ward, your nursling? Is not it time to go back for her?"

He was well aware at this moment that Laura was most thoroughly wearied herself, and that by a little contrivance he was secure of going alone to conduct the young nun home again.

"What! had you forgotten her?" said Laura.

"Could I think of more than one?" said Leslie, with a look of gentleness.

"And that one was of course absent," said Laura.

"Ah! I see," said Leslie, affecting a little pique, "that I am little understood. But at this moment," he added, quieting his voice, "however that may be, we must run back to take up our charge, for do you know what o'clock it is?"

Laura looked at her watch.

"Why did you allow me to forget time in this way?" said she.

"Was I likely to remind you?" said Leslie. "But at all events I will repair my error, at whatever sacrifice. I will force myself"—"from you," he thought of saying, but that was rather too strong an expression to come easily, so he began again—"I will force myself through the world of briars by the brook side, which will take me back to Miss Ladylift more quickly than the path we have followed, and I will bring her to join you by the garden road, which is, I suppose, the nearest way to the house. Even your delightful intrepidity would shrink from the brook side, and, indeed, should it be otherwise, I would not permit you to hazard yourself so perilously."

He was on his feet as he said this, and Laura, heated and wearied, could do nothing but agree; he looked back as he plunged into the thicket, and waving his hand, saw, and smiled to see, that she was waiting for some such token, and then sank upon the bench almost as weary as Elinor had been.

It was very easy for him to force his way along the brook, over great stones, and among tangled creepers and underwood; and indeed, his desire to reach the place where he had left Elinor, made these obstacles almost unperceived, and brought him, in a very short time, straight to the root-house in which they had parted from her. He hoped she would be panting with alarm, and crouching almost weeping for the want of some one to reassure her; certainly she would not have ventured back alone. Could he see her white dress? not yet, trees were in the way; he could not see it—she was not there—yes, yes, quite in the corner, there was some one. Now, how gently he would he comfort her, and she would cling to his arm.

But there was no such scene in store for him. Elinor, as though confiding in the assurance of safety she had received, had laid her cheek upon her arm and had fallen asleep. The shadow of the root-house had probably fostered the inclination of her eyes to close; her lips were parted, her hair pushed off her face, her colour heightened by the heat; she lay or reclined there, at rest, and Leslie paused suddenly as he perceived her sleeping figure. But the presence of a human being, the involuntary motions of life near her broke her slumber; she opened her eyes, and the habitual associations of her education, caused her a burst of alarm as she perceived who was so close to her. She sprang up and a step or two away from him.

"Oh, do not harm me!" she cried, involuntarily; then she collected her senses, and a deep blush spread over her face.

"I would die sooner than harm you!" cried Leslie, fervently; but approaching no nearer than where he stood when she sprang up.

"I came," he added, after a pause, "I came to be of use, if possible. Miss Chanson is gone home, and I will take you to her."

"You need not," said Elinor, "she told me the way was very easy to find—I can find the way."

"But, why should I not?" said Leslie. "I left Miss Chanson on purpose to be of use to you. She did not despise my services, and she thought you would not."

"Oh, I do not even think of such a word," said Elinor, coming a step nearer.

"That is the only feeling that can make you refuse so very common a service," said Leslie, trying to wear an air of proud humiliation.

"Indeed, indeed, not! but I did not know—I thought—I had better go home alone." So you had, innocent Elinor, but he cared not for that.

"If you so much dislike me as a companion," said Leslie, "I will go."

"I cannot dislike you," said Elinor; "it would be wrong to dislike anybody."

"I thought you did," said Leslie; "still, in order to be of any use to you, I came to see whether you were still here."

"That was good of you, very good, thank you," said Elinor; "it was doing me good even when you thought so ill of me—when you thought I was so unjust. Pray forgive me."

"Yes, surely," said Leslie, holding out his hand.

She looked him steadily in the face for a few seconds, and then took his hand.

"You cannot think I would harm you now," said Leslie; "what your Reverend Mother said in the Convent, did not mean me."

"No, you are not what she meant. She said I should be told of merits I had not, but you tell me of my faults."

"You see, then, that Miss Chanson and others, every one, in fact, is right in making me a companion. Till you came here nobody guessed it could be wrong. You have brought your own ideas among us."

"Oh, no, don't say that; I did not mean it. I did not know what people did here, that is all."

"Exactly," said Leslie; "and now shall we go home?"

"Yes, if you please," said Elinor. She took up her parasol and they walked leisurely along.

"You never," said her companion, "saw forests, and great open skies, and plains, in the Convent?"

"Never," said Elinor. "But we walked in the garden, and might sow flower seeds, and have beautiful flowers, and sometimes we went to the common, and the hill."

"Did you read sometimes of other fine things, such as these woods?"

"Yes."

"Are they like what you expected?"

"No, I did not know how beautiful they are."

"I should like to show you what I saw as I came up the brook," said Leslie; "you are not tired now, are you? Will you come a little out of the way?"

Elinor assented, eagerly, wishing to atone for having been tired once to-day. Leslie went off the path, and she followed, till the bank became steep and very inconvenient. Then he held out his hand and she leaned upon it as if it had been a helping stick; she wanted it again, up a few steep stones in the bank, and when she was at the top of those she came upon a sight which made her pluck away her hand altogether to fold both in speechless delight. The brook just in front of her came down under rocks which nearly met above it, and leaped about twenty feet from the edge of its bed to the pool below. The white foam, the graceful motion and shape, the sweet confusing sound, the freshness, took her very soul by surprise, and she was melted to tears.

"There—I knew I should give you pleasure," said Leslie; "that is why I brought you here."

"But so much pleasure is wrong, is not it?" said Elinor. "I learned in my lessons that St. Francis, when he crossed some mountains which were very beautiful, kept his eyes always on the ground not to see them."

Leslie did not say aloud, "Abject fool!" he said it only to himself; to Elinor he said, "I should think that very wicked, because his Creator offered him the pleasure, and he would not take it."

"What do you mean?". said Elinor, aghast. "It is the waterfall gives me pleasure."

"Still," said Leslie, "it has got no pleasure of its own."

"Has not it? yes—no—yes, it pleases me, it delights me."

"But it runs on day and night without being happy."

"That is because it is not alive."

"It runs over the rock because water must fall when it comes to a height, and it makes a noise because any one thing filling on another must make a noise, and the trees grow over it, because there were seeds from which they sprang; but they are all dead, as you say, and not happy. The pleasure is something different from all those things. It is in your mind. It is a gift to you, conveyed by things which have it not, and, therefore, a gift for which you ought to be grateful and use it."

"Could St. Francis be wrong?" said Elinor.

"Nay, I really think if you were to refuse to look at all this, you would be ungrateful to me, who brought you here, in the first place, and much more you ought to enjoy it, when you are so made that your nature is to enjoy."

"You think I may like it as much as I can?"

"Ay, freely, freely; whatever is pleasant is in your nature to enjoy."

"Whatever is pleasant?" said Elinor, reflecting on the many things, the late rising, the neglected task, the idle play, the lingering over her toilette, which were pleasant but which she had been told were wrong, and warned against the pleasure of them. Leslie enjoyed the confusion into which she was running.

"Why, so it seems to me," said he, with a candid tone.

Elinor was silent; he was no longer in haste to proceed, he lingered with her, teaching her that pleasure was her lawful guide; and when, at last, they went forward, moved as slowly as she was inclined to move and wore away the time, so that when they got back to the house, Laura had, long before, been compelled to give up waiting for them; had gone in alone, had been forced to preside over luncheon and to eat with the rest, or affect to eat, and after delaying to the utmost, had been driven from all excuses, and forced to bid the servants bring round, the carriage, previously ordered for an expedition. Just as she and her guests were going through the hall to set out, Mr. Leslie appeared alone coming up to the door. A sudden hope shot through Laura's heart that he had been alone since she left him. Elinor might have lost her way in the wood, but of course she would soon be found; and with all this unworded she accosted him.

"So; have you been looking for her all this time ......"

"For Miss Ladylift? oh, no'; I brought her home very slowly, for she was so much tired. She went through the breakfast parlour to her own room"

"Slowly, indeed!" said Laura, disdainfully; "you have been two hours and a half on the way."

"To me it seemed twice that," said Leslie, in a very low voice. Laura's lips relaxed by a line, no more.

"You will come with us?" said she, looking at the phaeton which followed the great barouche, and in which, if he liked, he might offer to drive her.

"That would be most delightful," said Leslie, "but I had not time for my letters this morning. I must write them to-day—besides I must get a crust of bread; besides I am in no condition to sit by the side of delicate silks. No, I must sacrifice that happiness."

Laura tossed her head, and turned away; and Leslie was very glad to have got off this tax upon him.

CHAPTER IV

Laura's anger and jealousy were almost more than she could bear. She learned to know that beating heart, that dry mouth, that distaste to food, that early waking and no more falling asleep, which make up the personal sufferings of mental anguish. She had to talk, to listen, to make music, while intensely preoccupied; and she had the pain of perceiving that Leslie grew more and more indifferent to keeping up the appearances of devotion to herself, and became, like her, absorbed by one object, but that object was not Laura Chanson.

Little incidents of this kind altered the position of the three persons whom we have presented to the reader. From a forlorn stranger, Elinor began to feel herself familiarised with persons and things, and to be aware that many were more favourable to her than the mistress of the house, whom she had looked upon as about to take the place of the Superior in her Convent.

Leslie, who had thought of nothing but amusing himself for a month or so, gradually found himself interested in a pursuit, which, at present, had the charm of novelty in the object, besides its difficulty. He reflected as little on the suffering he might inflict on the person to whom he had hitherto devoted himself, as on those which in future he might leave with the defenceless girl whom he at present worshipped; meantime, the suffering which Laura endured was very real, whether she were justified in having exposed herself to it or not. The young girl who had unconsciously taken her place was hateful to Laura; it was difficult to keep up the appearance of interest and tender protection which had been their first relation to each other. She justified her altered feelings to herself by saying that severity was necessary to teach Elinor something of the ways of the world she had to move in, and to correct the mistakes into which her Convent life led her; and, in fact, Elinor had great need of superintendence; for with all her early impressions wrecking around her, she did not know to what to cling, or where to stop, or how go back. They had laughed at her prudery, and in the innocence of her nature she did not now know what difference to make between Leslie and Laura; between Mr. Chanson, her elderly guardian, and Leslie, her young adorer. That Leslie was more good-natured to her than anybody else she was certain, and if she wanted any advice or service, she supposed that she might as well ask him for either; not to ask him would show that long-taught horror of man which she haft just recently been made ashamed of.

In this embarrassment of perception she, one morning, brought into the library a heavy packet, containing letters which she had written to her Convent; and the first person from whom she made an inquiry how to effect its transmission, was Laura. But Laura was supercilious.

"Leave it on the table, child, with the other letters. There is no need to make a fuss about posting a letter."

Elinor coloured and did as she was bid. But she was not satisfied, and after a short, silent bit of doubt, she looked round for some kinder listener, and turning her shy eyes to Mr. Leslie, saw that though he had a book in his hand, and his head was bent towards it, he was, in fact, looking at her. Elinor's colour rose again, for shame that she had been ashamed to appeal at once to him; and avoiding the appearance of mistrust for which she had been laughed at, she smiled directly that she caught his glance, and went up to him as if he had been Sister Françoise or Sister Jeanne, and in a very low voice asked him what she should do. He was fully disposed to make it a serious affair, that he might be able to confer an obligation by arranging it, and rising, took it (Elinor following him) into the recess of the window and there examined the packet.

"It will not go by the post without a little trouble," said he; "it weighs, I should think, six ordinary letters."

"I dare say; for I have written to so many of them," said Elinor.

"It must be paid before it leaves England," said Leslie. "The postman will not know how much to charge. We ought to put it into the office ourselves."

"How can I do that? It is so far to the town," said Elinor.

"Is not it possible Miss Chanson may intend to drive or ride there?" suggested Leslie.

"Shall I ask her?"

"Do;" and he watched her timid advance to Laura, whom she instinctively began to feel was not likely to look very benignantly on a request of her's.

"No, it's not possible," he heard Laura say, and he concluded that she had heard the words which he himself had used. Laura said nothing more, for or against, and went on reading her book, the pages of which she turned tempestuously. Elinor said nothing, but again looked to Leslie, who, by a gesture, invited her to return to the window.

"If you will trust me," said he, "I have thought how to manage it; since there is no chance of Miss Chanson going to the post town, I will ride over there at once, and if I go quickly, I shall be in time for the foreign mail which goes out this morning."

"Does it?" said Elinor.

"Yes, I feel quite sure of that, and I will post and pay your letter, and make it quite sure of reaching the hands of these dear Sisters."

"Oh, will you?" said Elinor; "how very good-natured you are. Only do you not want to do something else? I am afraid this is so much trouble."

"No, a pleasure," said Leslie; then moderating his tone, he added, "I like an early ride; I want one to put me in high force this morning."

"That's very lucky," said the literal Elinor. "Tell me what it will cost," and she took out her purse. Leslie's heart smote him he saw that slender purse so slenderly provided. It was too much in keeping with the defenceless state and nature of that fair piece of human porcelain.

"Oh, not much. I will take care it goes safely."

"But I must pay it," said Elinor, earnestly. "The Reverend Mother told me never to run in debt, especially ……"

"To the monster man," said Leslie, finishing the phrase she broke off, and smiling.

Elinor again was ashamed of a good lesson. She did not know what guidance to follow; plainly she felt herself laughed at, and that was painful. She slid back her purse into the pocket of her apron, and stood again like a puzzled, penitent child.

"Such a nothing of a debt," said Leslie, "only give me the letter." He took it, and moving away to Mr. Chanson's room, which opened from the library, asked him if he could have a horse, and then returning, told Laura he was going to Cantleton and inquired if he could do anything for her.

"I thought," said Laura, smiling painfully, "we were all to ride to the Hollow Glen."

"True, I had forgotten; but it will make no difference will it, if I am absent?"

"None," said Laura, "of course. One's guests, of course, amuse themselves if their host cannot do it."

Leslie gave a deprecating "No, no;" and added, "Guests who do that, are not worthy of being received; but I really have a little business."

Laura laughed scornfully, she could not repress her irritation. "Selfish business, purely?" said she, interrogating.

Elinor heard all this and was very much grieved that his good-nature to her should bring this reproach upon him. She knew it was wrong to let another suffer in one's place and spoke bravely out.

"He is not selfish, he is going to take care of my letter."

Leslie himself coloured at this sudden shifting of the ground under his feet, and Laura burst into that insolent laugh which bows down all but such as can laugh insolently in return. The moisture which precedes tears came into Elinor's eyes. She turned partly away, and Leslie could not but gaze on the innocent pretty picture she made.

"Don't let me detain you, Mr. Letter-carrier" said Laura. "I was not aware of your new office. You came here as an independent gentleman, but a new character ......"

"Does what?" said Leslie, after a silent pause.

"Nay, nothing at all—only I thought you were not listening to me, your attention seemed elsewhere."

"Oh! don't doubt that whatever Miss Chanson says, or even hints, has my best attention and consideration. I'll go now—pray excuse me."

"By all means. I wish you to ...... do as you like," said Laura, abruptly; and he saw her lip tremble.

"Poor Elinor!" thought he, looking back, "what will you make of the scolding you are about to get." And a scolding it was, indeed. Not that Laura intended it when she began, but she lost her self-command as she talked; and the anguish which she endured, through Elinor, made her blind to the innocence, and deaf to the guileless purity of the young girl.

"I don't know, Elinor," she began, "whether you think it quite proper to send one's acquaintances all over the country on your errands; for my part, I know I should be heartily ashamed of doing so."

"Oh, my dear Miss Chanson, was it wrong?"

"Heartily ashamed, that's all I can say; and so would any one with the least sense of decency," said Laura, beginning to tremble. "But you have your own notions, doubtless."

"No, indeed, indeed!"

"And to give yourself such airs in another person's house—commanding everything as if it were your own, and more than if it were your own. The horses, the servants, the very guests, all to be at your command. You are to send our guests just to carry your letters to the post. I think what serves our letters might serve yours."

"I wish I had known—I am very, very sorry."

"What made you fix on Mr. Leslie for your confidant, pray. Was it because you found him here, interested ...... I mean that you thought him not likely to devote himself sufficiently to your superior merits, unless specially invited. You need not cry, it is no use to pretend one thing and do another; men are always taken in by anybody who gives themselves the trouble, and for my part, I warn you that they will only despise you, they will find out ..... in fact, I see through you as if you were glass."

"I wish I could see myself and know how I have offended you," said Elinor, weeping.

"Me offended! oh, dear me, not I! Mr. Leslie is as perfectly indifferent to me, as you are. I only warn you for your own sake that you are acting as not another young girl in all the whole of England would dare to act."

So saying, Laura fled from the room, for she could contain herself no longer; and while Elinor wept silently in the library, Laura sobbed aloud in her boudoir, the door of which she had banged behind her and fastened with a double turn of the key.

Elinor had a guiltless conscience in her favour, and recovered first; but she was very unhappy, and being ignorant as to what she had done wrong she resolved first to beg Mr. Leslie's pardon, and then to entreat his assistance in explaining to her the course of conduct which would be doing right. She stole up the back staircase to her room; bathed her face as she had often done in the pupils' room in the Convent, when she had been scolded and wanted to avoid the imputation of resenting the scolding; and putting on her bonnet and gray cloak, went dejectedly down again, and glided by the most sequestered ways she could find, towards the gate of the park by which she believed Mr. Leslie would return. Here she sat down, patiently to wait for him, and screened herself from observation by choosing her seat among some drooping elms, whose long branches, as one sees sometimes with the elm tree, had turned downwards soon after leaving the stem, and bowed themselves to the ground, as if kneeling.

But, patient as she was, and used to waiting, the length of time she remained there, during which there was nothing coming, made her first uneasy, and at last anxious. She got up and walked into the road, whence she could command a long sight of the highway beyond the gates, and still, when all was blank, returned to her seat, and resumed the paper-mark she was plaiting in the shape of a cross. The woman who kept the lodge had seen this manœuvre more than once, and at last, in the civility of her heart, came out as Elinor again looked down the road, and asked if she was pleased to be waiting for some body.

"No," said Elinor; "only I think Mr. Leslie will return this way from Cantleton;" and as she said his name, she blushed deeply as young girls will do, at sight or at speaking of a young acquaintance of the opposite sex, though as heart-whole as a bird just fledged, on the edge of its nest.

The old woman laughed in a motherly way. "Oh! that's it," said she. "I did not know, miss; you will be pleased to forgive me," and she withdrew to her cottage, and Elinor to her tree, puzzled again, and but half liking what she did not understand in the old woman.

It was an hour and a half after she had come to the spot, when she heard the trot of horses' feet, at which her heart gave a bound, but directly the sound of wheels became audible, and the next bound of her heart was what might be called in the opposite direction. She went further under the trees, and saw Laura and others on horseback, and a carriage following, all making towards the Lodge at a good, exhilarating pace. As they approached it, she perceived Mr. Leslie coming in the opposite direction, and both parties stopped and had some communion together. What they said she did not know, but she perceived some laughter, some gestures of expostulation, and that Laura, after great apparent earnestness, suddenly jerked away her horse, and set off at an actual gallop; while Mr. Leslie, who she supposed had refused their invitation to join them, waved his hand to them, and came alone, and slowly, along the road in the park.

Without the least hesitation. or embarrassment, Elinor came forward from the trees, and caught his sight, making a motion inviting him to speak to her. He immediately rode up to the place where she stood, and dismounting, eagerly told her what he really had done, and a great deal more which he claimed to have done for her. Elinor was more and more troubled, and as soon as he would hear her, professed her regret at having thus employed him, in so penitent a manner, that the tears again rose to her eyes, and in his heart arose a tender pity, which made him ready to fall down at her feet, and raise her by his humble love above all claim and all necessity for pity.

"I who have been so happy to be employed by you! who felt it such a kindness on your part to a man who has no friends, who wants so much a little sympathy, who would be glad to earn a kind 'Thank you' at any sacrifice, much more by the merest commonplace service. Ah, Miss Ladylift! ah, Elinor! do not talk so, do not think in this way. Who can have led you to such thoughts?"

"Alas! Miss Chanson was very angry with me. She told me no girl in England would be so bold, especially with you."

"Did she; was it any consideration for me. Did she tell you that it was from consideration—from any regard to me, then?"

"No! no! She said she did not care for you—it was all on my own account."

"Ha! ha!" said Leslie, "she said so. Then I think it is time for me to go away."

"You go away! are you then really angry with me?"

"Oh! I beseech you, do not say, do not think such harsh, hard words," said Leslie, taking her hand, and gently leading her further into the wood.

They walked on together side by side, deeply engaged in conversation, in which Elinor's defencelessness touched Leslie's heart with more of good emotion than he had known could dwell there. Yet he enjoyed involving her in a situation which depended upon himself to make it safe or dangerous, and which, at all events, was one in which she compromised herself with the prudent, and those who had more habit of the world than she. He perceived her perfect innocence of every such notion, and was every moment renewing a compact with himself to hold her in reverence. Yet he secured her hand on his arm—he could not keep himself from touching the fingers that lay there, from gently pressing the arm which touched his own. A trifling circumstance did more to check him than all his good resolutions. This was his horse, whose bridle he held, and whose uneven pace had constantly to be regulated; sometimes it would start forward, and annoy its master with a threatened invasion of his toes; sometimes stop to snatch at a bough, and when jerked on again, would shake its head, and flourish in the air in a manner dangerous to its safe keeping by the bridle.

Elinor's attention was diverted from her own griefs, and Leslie's sympathy, by the manœuvres of the horse. With the tears in her eyes, she was provoked to laughter at its perversity; and when most grateful for Leslie's assurance of friendship and support, could not help turning their talk to the horse's entertaining movements. Leslie hated the animal; and, at last, to keep the conversation in the train which pleased him, he invited Elinor to sit down beneath a tree far and deep in the wood; where, having fastened his tiresome animal to one at a distance, he returned and placed himself by her, distant from all the eyes that should have been guarding her, and undefended by any inward consciousness of being where she needed defence.

"When I am gone," he said, "and go I must, will you think of me?—will you remember the friend to whom you can always apply?"

"Yes, yes!" said Elinor; "there is no danger that I should do otherwise, for it is you only who tell me what I ought to do, who show me kindly where I am wrong."

"And if you want advice," said Leslie—and there he hesitated, whether indeed to ask her to enter into secret correspondence with him.

"I can write to you, if you will tell me your direction," said Elinor.

"Divine Elinor!" cried Leslie, carried away with delicious surprise; and suddenly lifting the hand he held to his lips, he kissed it fervidly, so that in astonishment she drew it away, and a smile came for an instant over her mouth.

Leslie looked down at her with delight; he drew still nearer to her, when the sound of rustling boughs smote his ear, and then the voice of the Squire—of Mr. Chanson, of Elinor's guardian—broke upon them.

"Hey!—what's this? You and Miss Ladylift out in the wood, here?"—he was not a man of words.

Leslie started up; Elinor kept her seat.

"Yes; I came this way to enjoy the shade, and Miss Ladylift had done the same. I met with her a moment ago, and was about to show her the nearest way home."

Elinor listened with wonder. She thought certainly Leslie had forgotten that she had come to meet him near the lodge, and that they had spent an hour in walking to the spot together, without any reference to going home; however, she heard him as children hear their elders say things they have themselves been taught not to say, and unconsciously they take a lesson in the difference between learning and practising.

Mr. Chanson asked no more; he only held out his arm to her, and said,

"Come home with me. Laura ought to have been with you." He had a fishing-rod in the other hand, and had been making his way to the brook.

"Miss Chanson is out riding," said Elinor.

"And why did not you go? What made you wander to this out-of-the-way place?"

Elinor hesitated; she did not like to say she had been scolded, and had crept away.

Mr. Chanson thought she had made an appointment with Leslie, and that her embarrassment came from that consciousness.

"Well, well!" said he. "Mr. Leslie, you had better look after your horse. That's your best way home—along the green path, there. I'll take her over the brook by the foot-bridge. Now then!"

And he walked forward, Elinor very willing to go with him, but looking back to see how Leslie got up to the horse, which was drawing away, and shying at his approach.

"Never mind that," said the Squire; "you must not be wandering about in this style. I'll talk to Laura."

CHAPTER V

Leslie had become aware that his presence had become unacceptable to the mistress of the house, or rather that his behaviour made it so, and therefore that it was time he should go. Her evident pique, which he had understood from Elinor's report of her conversation with Laura, had confirmed this resolution, and he had determined to "have found letters at Cantleton" which required his presence elsewhere, even before the Squire looked so grim at him for being alone with Elinor in the wood.

At dinner, therefore, he avoided sitting by Elinor, made himself as agreeable to Laura as her anger would allow, and before the ladies withdrew, told her he must leave Chanson Wood next morning. Laura believed not one word of the story of the letters. She had heard her brother's report, and when he upbraided her with neglect of her charge, had given him to understand that the young girl chose to manage her own concerns, and was amenable neither to reproof nor persuasion. The Squire had guilelessly believed her, inclined the more to do so by what he had himself remarked; and Laura, strong in the impression she had then made, had courage to attempt the same thing with Leslie.

"I am sorry," said she, with a voice in which it was easy to perceive emotion, for his departure touched the sorest place in her heart, "I am very sorry that you have found reason to leave us."

"Indeed, so am I. I have enjoyed the visit so much, that it is odious to me to learn from my letters ...... "

"From them all?" said Laura, smiling sadly enough. "No, no! it's not your letters."

"And what is it, then?" said Leslie, abruptly, and colouring.

"Why should not you treat me as a friend?" said Laura. "But I have no right to intrude on your secrets."

"I've no secrets," said Leslie, mounting higher on his high horse.

"I will not ask any," said Laura; "only I cannot bear to see a friend I value suffering from capricious power."

"You speak in enigmas," said Leslie. "I am not suffering at all, that I know of, except in leaving you."

"That's unkind," said Laura, suddenly, and thrown off her guard; "that's the last of your thoughts. I only wish you were as little deceived as you deceive me."

"Deceived—deceit!" said Leslie'; "what are we talking about? I leave two friends here, who are, I know, as true as the mirror of a mountain lake; two charming ladies, whose friendship is the pride of my life— Miss Chanson and her ward, to whose joint society I offer up all my homage."

Laura looked at him steadily for a few seconds, and then changing her manner suddenly, uttered her scornful laugh, which made the blood tingle in his face as though he had been detected in the most egregious simplicity.

"I doubt nothing, I doubt nobody," said he. "I am the simplest fellow in the world. When I see blue sky, I believe it blue."

"And the little angels and all?" said Laura.

"Certainly."

"I'll say nothing against it, then;" and slightly shrugging her shoulders, she escaped.

When he took leave of the Squire it was the same thing.

"You are going away in a hurry," said Mr. Chanson. "Have you had a tiff with anybody?"

"By no means. I have business which obliges me ......"

"Ay, ay. They'll miss you, especially the little girl there; but mind you, I know nothing about her, beyond that I must take care of her. She has not a penny, and I am afraid is whimmy."

Leslie was vexed at the Squire's caution. Laura's would have been nothing, had not her brother's confirmed it. There must be something, as both had made a similar observation. Yet, when he met Elinor before breakfast next morning, walking in the garden, and she told him that she had hoped to see him there, and it was therefore she had come, he forgot to ask himself if such child-like simplicity could be feigned, and renewed all those vows of friendship and support which Elinor needed; and vowswarmer than which he felt instinctively would not be understood. His intention was to leave her for a time, since his hostess took his desertion so much amiss, but if his own heart preserved the impression Elinor had made upon it, he had resolved to see her again at any cost, and then to let the course of events determine their future relations.

Accordingly he betook himself home, where he had occupation and amusement awaiting him, and where the novelty of being master gave him interests which made it the place most frequently in his thoughts when absent. It was an ancient house, which seemed, from the remains of building about it, to have been once a portion of a much larger residence. It stood in a valley, upon an isolated hill, on the slopes of which the various ruined walls, covered for the most part with the vegetation of years, and crowned with mountain ash and birch, offered many a romantic seat, and many a sheltered bit of terrace for whole natural beds of wild flowers. The house was out of order, but not ruinous, and offered scope to the eye and fancy of the proprietor as to its restoration to a beautiful and convenient dwelling. From it one looked down the valley to the church, with its spire rising above the cottages and orchards of a village, and on the stream which wound its way through wood and meadow, wandering on towards hills, for ever varying in light and shade, and as it had a western aspect, offering every evening the gorgeous spectacle of sunset.

All this valley belonged to Leslie, and so did the neighbouring lands, for about 3,000 acres in all, of poor but lovely country. He had a neighbour, richer than himself, and with a grander place, to the east of his valley; and a few other scattered houses, together with a market town about six miles on, over the common and heathy grounds, made up his neighbourhood. There was plenty of game on Leslie's estate, and one plan for this autumn was to amuse himself with its pursuit; but though he was as active as might reasonably be guessed from his admirable frame, he had never got up to any enthusiasm for hunting or shooting. He tried the latter the first morning after his return, but though the partridges were plentiful, and his success considerable, he thought it a more stupid occupation than ever, to-day.

While he was walking over the dry stubbles, what was Elinor doing? Was she reading one of those little dreamy books which he had commented upon many a time, till an unwilling smile broke over her lips, and she turned away her face that he might not see it? or was she suffering from Laura's bad temper, with that pretty mournful expression in her eyes and on her mouth, which made her look even younger than her own fresh youth? Was she sitting, cool and pale, on the fallen oak in the wood, while he was toiling, hot and red, in company with his gamekeeper, watching a dog beguiling a bird?

He went home very early, and then walked about his own place, cutting away boughs which shut out the lovely view, and projecting how to convert into an entrance a hexagon room supported by a central pillar, which was said once to have been a chapel.

But he was constantly leaning the hatchet idle against a tree, or drawing scrolls and scrawls on the margin of the paper where he was making his plans—his thoughts being elsewhere, at the side of Elinor, thinking over something said or done by her, and what he had said, or had better have said or done, in return.

Two or three days made his home intolerable—intolerable, at least, to a man so free to go whithersoever his wishes directed him—and getting up one morning at dawn, from a bed where he could not sleep, he put up a portmanteau before his servant was awake, and by the time the labourers came to their work, was driving to the little neighbouring town where the coach changed horses at seven o'clock. Nobody asked, and nobody knew where he was going: he went quite alone, and by one change of vehicle and another reached the neighbourhood of Chanson Wood by nightfall.

He would not on any account have been recognised; he was ashamed of returning so soon, and took the most genuine precautions to remain in obscurity. He engaged a room a couple of miles from the park, at a little public house where, having never entered it during his visit to the Squire, he was unknown; and pretending something about an engagement to survey the country, and displaying some paper and pencils, felt himself safe from inquiry.

The intense desire to see Elinor again, however, would not let him rest in the house, and as soon as the night was quite dark, he took his way along the lane, and through the wicket beside the carriage entrance, and then by cautious approaches to that side of the house where was the room the family occupied in the evening. All was carelessly secure, as in a great country house in the midst of its gardens, and inhabited by its multitude; and he had but to push open the low iron gate in the fence between the garden and the park, to find himself upon the walk which led up beneath the windows. There was a flower border, and then a green sward, between the house and the gravel walk, so that Leslie, by walking on the turf, and then on the silent mould of the border, got noiselessly up to an open sash, and could look in and command the whole room.

All was silent inside. There were three persons, and one was Elinor. She was sitting beside a lamp, with her face to the window, but it was leant over a piece of work which she held in her hands. There was nothing but white of different shades about her; her muslin gown was white, a white satin bow fastened it at her throat, a white lace border, or collar, lay flat on her low shoulders, the work in her hands was white cambric, which she was embroidering; her pale face and fair hands were touched by the lamplight, and her motionless figure seemed patient of a dull employment and ungenial companions.

Laura reclined in a chair, partly turned from the window, reading; and the Squire was fast asleep on a sofa, breaking the silence by regular snoring, loud enough to increase Leslie's chance of escaping detection. He saw her then, he could speak to her with silently moving lips, he could appeal to her with passionate eyes and entreating hands, he could bend his knee towards the ground, adoring her beauty, or rather her loveableness. Perhaps he a little over-wrought these gesticulations, for while most wrapped in them, a little dog, which was lying with its back well into Laura's silk gown, jumped up, and gave a sharp volley of barks.

Elinor looked suddenly up, but Leslie was gone into the shadow. The Squire did not cease his sonorous aspirations, and Laura was too much used to her Spitz's hysterical alarms to move so much as her head. But Leslie felt his security gone; and that probably the little Spitz's eyes were even then on the window, beaming with the purpose of another frantic yap upon the smallest sign from outside. He withdrew very cautiously, but his soul was bitter against the Spitz.

"Let me catch you outside these walls, Master Puff, and see if you disturb me again," murmured he, as he retreated.

The necessity of his soul was to see Elinor again; he wished to be the unseen spectator of what she was and did, to make sure that a creature so innocent really existed, and to enjoy the spectacle if it was true. To enjoy it and destroy it; for he looked no further than to present gratification of the passion which filled his breast—all his remoter thoughts were of ambition and success in the tempestuous world, which seemed another sphere from that he occupied at present.

He put on, next day, the dress of a workman, and as deeply slouched a hat as he could suppose consistent with the character. He provided himself with an axe, and hoped to pass unrecognised, if he could avoid direct communication with his former host and fellow guests; and taking his way into the woods about the house, went first to the brook, where he had shown Elinor the waterfall, and where he knew she had occasionally resorted after that time.

His expectations were more than fulfilled, for he had no pains of waiting to go through, no fears, no doubtful hopes; a figure was standing on the very spot whither he had led Elinor, and though the face was turned away, the elegant shape was that which he longed to see. The falling water prevented his step from being heard, and he was able to take up a place among the trees, where he could observe her, yet run scarce any danger of detection. Should she perceive him, he would deal a few strokes at the trees, and trust to be taken for the forester, and pass unnoticed.

The unconscious Elinor made her preparations for passing the burning hours in shade and a refreshing atmosphere. She laid aside her bonnet, put by her gloves, unfastened the cotton gown from her throat, and it charmed him to see she did not open a book, but unfolded a piece of household work, and industriously shaped, and hemmed, and sewed at the white jacket she was making. Sometimes she paused, and looked long at the lovely fall of waters, and once going down to the edge of the brook, took water in her joined hands, and drank from that pretty cup. Then returning, she resumed her work, and gave no sign of thoughts within, except a few times singing some notes, like a bird alone in the sun, trying a passage taught by the impulse of its melodious throat.

It was a fair picture of still life, and he looked at it with the passion of a lover, and the eye of an artist; but at last he began to grow discontented that there was no sign of wanting or thinking of him, no looks cast upwards, no sighs, no restless movement, which he might have interpreted into regret that he was not there. Should he suddenly appear, would he be welcome even? Yes, welcome, perhaps, as a novelty, not as the thing desired—welcome to come and go, but if she knew he had come all that way merely to look at her, she would laugh. He was a very young man, and little knew the patience of a modest maiden, nor the absence of all spoken words, and speaking signs, when she is with herself alone, and is occupied with her natural duties and works.

He watched her all that morning, and saw her at last fold her work, rise and gather some beech leaves while she stood under the tree, to wind one into the other, till they made a wreath, then hanging it on her wrist, she took up her wicker basket, and shortly withdrew towards the house.

"Dear household Lar," said he, coming and standing exactly in front of the seat she had occupied, "one day you will sit beside some humble hearth, content to do the lowly offices of home, to live the joyless life of little wants and coarse means; your fragile loveliness will be stained by weather and hard work, your pure voice will have lost its clearness, but neither you nor yours will think it worsened since these days. I should not love you then—I shall be in my grave, or on the summit of ambition then—but there is an interval between that time and this, in which, oh! Elinor! your quiet heart must beat—beat as mine does now—in which you must know the agony of my adoration—in which we must make life all diamond-light, if it be but for the space of a moon's change! Exquisite calm face, when will you lighten thus for me?"

Next day, he came again, and saw her again. It was, as the village bells told him, a Saint's day, and Elinor, whom no one helped to perform her usual devotions in an appointed place, came into the entangled woods to find a temple. He saw her kneel in front of the great tree, and with humble eyes cast upon the ground, sign the cross upon her bosom, and open her little book of prayer.

Even in these devotions there was something which suited his feeling about Elinor better than if the prayer had been more untaught, more her own creation. She passively did what she had been taught to do—she murmured over a form of words, continually coming to the same repetition, and making the same sign of devotion. She turned her pages to the places where marks in the book showed she ought to go, and though the service lasted long, showed no wish either to shorten or prolong it, but did what was set down for her, and then rose roase and had done.

Again she took her seat upon the fallen tree, again unfolded her work, and again, with the shadows of boughs and leaves moving over her as the breath of air gently swayed them, sat plying her household needle. What thoughts broke in upon the even train which was necessary to guide that needle, he would fain have guessed. Surely some thoughts must accompany the motion of those active fingers— perhaps there were many given to convent days; perhaps some to him—he wished it, but hardly hoped it; but at last, without the sewing being interrupted, he heard well known notes begin to murmur from her throat, and go on to a continued but still low song, which made him believe those tranquil thoughts had indeed been recalling him, and had come to the point which made that song and him one common subject, for it was the air of a duett in which he had attempted to join her, an air sung at village weddings in Brittany, and he had never seen her laugh so cordially as at his failures in trying to keep a second. Now he heard the village notes and verses again, and believed his own image was before her.

"Nous sommes venus vous voir,
Du fond de not'e village,
Pour vous complimenter
Sur vot'e mariage
A monsieur votre epoux,
Aussi bien comme à vous," &c.

She broke off before the verse was finished, and he saw her look from her work, and though he could not hear it, was certain she laughed—briefly, as one does alone. Then there was some measuring or adapting in the work, which took up her attention, and obliged her to rise and use the fallen tree for a table, and when all was in order, she again sat down to work, and seemed to have forgotten all about "vot'e mariage." Probably they were the words in the song which were the very last she thought about.

The intense pleasure of watching, and appropriating her solitary ways and movements, had gone on long past mid-day, when Leslie heard a step coming along the rough track which led from the wood walk to this unfrequented place. It was only a servant, who, approaching Elinor, delivered some message and went away again; and she, in consequence it seemed, collected the materials of her employment, and left her seat probably to obey a summons to the house. Leslie was vexed, first at losing his amusement, and next at the way in which it was lost.

"I thought he had chosen a spot all unknown," said he, to himself—"one which a lover only could discover—but it seems the very servants know where she is to be found, much more every idle puppy and loiterer belonging to the society"—puppy himself, though of a stout, handsome breed.

However, there was no probability of her return, he thought, and after half an hour's waiting for the chance of it, he had moved away, and was descending towards the brook, when he perceived a motion in the boughs overhanging the path, and stopping to watch, perceived it was Elinor coming again, and in haste, to the accustomed spot. Leslie was in front of her, and accident gave him a better place to see her than he had ventured to choose for himself; his fear was that she should also perceive him, but she evidently was in a mood so preoccupied as not readily to have her attention caught by outer objects. All her humble tranquillity was gone. As soon as she reached her fallen tree, she sank down upon it, and leaning both hands upon one of the projecting branches, hid her face, and wept bitterly. She lifted her head more than once, to wipe her streaming eyes, and then hid them again, as though the lovely scene were blotted and rendered null by the grief within.

Presently she rose, and went hastily down to the brook, and there kneeling and stooping over it, dashed the water repeatedly over her face, and let her hair come dripping from the stream. She then sat down on a rock close to the margin, and not five yards from Leslie, but, as it chanced, with her back to him, and bringing from a little basket a case containing paper and a pen, she put her lithe figure into such a position as to find a desk on part of the rock where she sat, and began hastily to write.

Leslie's heart beat faster than ever. Had she not asked him for his direction, that she might apply to him if ever she was in trouble? Was she writing to him? To whom else was it probable, that in that sudden grief, whatever it might be, she should be writing? and he so near—he could almost see the lines as she traced them. Did she summon him to her? What would she say if he were suddenly at her side?—but then he should lose all the gratitude due to obeying her call—he should be the inferior who had come to seek, instead of the superior who had been besought to come. No, he would not hazard that!—besides, he was not sure that she was writing to him; it might be some one else to whom she was appealing. She had very suddenly made him her confidant—it was not impossible that there might be others equally favoured. What was it the Squire had said she was—whimmy?—he had called her whimmy. Yet, alas! that she should cry so, and no one be near to comfort her. Would not she cling to him like a friend if she saw him? would not she be gladder than she knew? Yet, possibly, no!—he would not hazard it—but that letter he would get by some means, and it should not be long before it was his; then he should know what to do.

Meantime, Elinor finished the hastily-written letter, folded it, and replacing the little matters in her basket, pushed the basket among the ferns and stones, and hastily took her way by a difficult path down the dingle. Leslie concluded that she was going to the post-office to put in her letter; and he purposed to follow soon after, and ask for it in his own name, in case it should be addressed to him. But then the letter would be directed to his own place, of which he had given Elinor the direction, and at the post-office they would not dare give it except where it was addressed. Yet he knew the old woman who acted as post-mistress, and she had been constantly in the habit of seeing him during his visit at Mr. Chanson's, and perhaps, if he resumed the clothes and character of Mr. Leslie, she might be prevailed upon to disregard the direction in favour of the bodily presence of the man directed to. He therefore rushed back to his lodgings to change his peasant's dress, and then, regardless of being discovered, regardless of everything except the possession of the letter, he turned back boldly to the post-office. For the convenience of the great house, it was located at the park gates, in the lodge, and was kept by the same old woman who had taken notice of Elinor's watch for Mr. Leslie. She was perfectly familiar with his appearance, but when he went into the house and inquired if there was anything for him, she started as if she had no expectation nor wish to see him, and seemed to take the circumstance occurring as a personal injury.

"A letter for P. Leslie, Esq.?" said she; "there's more fuss than enough about P. Leslie, Esq. I can't sit to my tea for people all coming for that blessed letter."

"Then there is one," cried Leslie, eagerly, "give it."

"I did not say there was," said the old woman; "and if there should be, it's gone away in the west bag as directed."

"Gone!" cried he, stamping impatiently; "what luck I have! but when—there's been no mail since—when did it go, I say?"

"The mail was due at eleven and half," said the post-mistress, "but it might be ten minutes later."

"You are not telling me the truth," said Leslie; "the letter was not here then."

"If you know better than I, sir, then I say no more."

"Nay!" said Leslie; "but you know you were telling stories—and what's the use? The letter is here, and you may as well get half a guinea by giving it me as not."

"I can't do no such thing; it's made up in the bag to go where it ought to go, and I'm forbidden by my office to let anybody meddle with it, except the right person at the right place."

"But," said Leslie, "you have already let somebody meddle; the person—the people—who you say have been disturbing you at your tea."

The old woman coloured up to the eyes, though she would not give way. "I said somebody disturbed me; and so she did. Was not the hole cut away in the window for letters to be dropped in? Where's the use of bringing them into the house, and not being content with the natural gap."

"That's not what you meant by disturbing you," said Leslie; "that person may have brought the letter into the house, but after it was in the box, I believe you have been taking it out for somebody else, and you can't produce it for the right owner."

"Can't I?" said the old woman.

"No! I shall inform against you," said. Leslie, "for allowing your office to be tampered with, unless you immediately put it into my possession."

"That will just be doing the thing you are going to complain of," said the old woman.

Leslie was provoked to smile."Come, come," said he, "I will have the letter, and you may as well take my money at once, for the trouble of opening your bags, although I know they are not shut. Here, old lady, don't tell any more lies, but do as you are bid."

The ancient post-mistress laughed, and went to the box into which the letters were dropped. Leslie found out her fibs as fast as she composed them, and she acknowledged him a master spirit. A little rummaging and a little grumbling produced the letter in question, and Leslie seizing it, first of all before devouring the contents, carefully examined the folds and fastening, for he had conceived certain suspicions from the old lady's words.

"Who opened this letter?" said he, abruptly, after looking at it attentively.

"Nobody but yourself," said she, trying to lay her thumb on the fastening; "you have worried it in turning it about so."

"No, no!" said Leslie, guarding it from her, for though he had only asked the question as a random shot, he now was certain that there was some mystery.

"That I have not, neither shall you; but you shall tell me what I ask, for I have you in my power, and I will know."

The old sharpshooter was chased from her defences, but ran and took up another position. "Well—well," said she, "you are a young gentleman, and a mighty good-looking, and if I were you, I should not take it amiss that the ladies thought worth while escorting my letters, and jealousing what was writ in them. It is not old gentlemen and old ladies as do such things."

"In short, Miss Chanson has had this letter in her hands before me."

"Oh! dear me!—Miss Chanson!—no, dear no!—I never said no such thing."

"No, you did not say it!" said Leslie. "I perfectly comprehend that it could not possibly be that lady; and now don't be afraid, for I know all I want. Good evening."

"That's a wilful man," said the post-mistress to herself, "and those be two silly girls to have anything to do with him."

Leslie meantime walked hastily away, and took a path over the fields to be out of observation, opening and reading the much canvassed letter as he went along. He could not but smile at the simplicity of the writer's alarms, and of her confidence in him.

"Sir, ("that's Monsieur," said he)—

"SIR—You are my only friend; I do not know what to do unless you can help me—and you told me to ask you for help if I was in trouble. Have you money you can lend me? I will pay you back, a little every quarter, and once you said it was not wrong to borrow from you. Miss Chanson called me, and gave me many bills, which I did not know of—perhaps they will put me in prison. What will become of me?

"ELINOR LADYLIFT."

"Poor, precious, enchanting Elinor!" cried he; "how unkind, how sententious, they are to you. I can see the matter from here; ordinary bills are thrust into your hands, without explanation, without advice, and your conventual imagination sees nothing in them but an ogre of a creditor, and dungeons and chains. Oh! how can I be soonest with you? I dare not come at once, for even your innocence would disbelieve that I was as far off as I ought to have been when I got your summons. Yet—summons! no, it is not that; nothing was further, I do believe, from your thoughts, than to call me to you—yet, poor dove, you have done so, and when such fair birds are no better looked after by their natural guardians, what is indeed to become of them? Now I must write so as not to frighten her."

Accordingly he wrote in the soberest manner, making much, indeed, of her embarrassments, but promising to alleviate them; and then informed her "that particular circumstances having called him into her neighbourhood, he had received her letter in a most fortunately brief space of time, and he should be able, that very evening, to meet her near the waterfall in the wood, and to bring her the means of extricating herself from her difficulties."

"She will wonder why I should not walk straight up to the house, and ask to see Miss Ladylift," said he, as he sealed his letter; "but I hope the spirit of intrigue and coquetry may awaken in her sufficiently to do as I suggest, and ask no questions."

The next difficulty was to convey this letter to her, and it perplexed him till he saw the Squire and Laura ride past his lodging, and thus knew they were out of the way; and then he resolved to go himself to the house, in the peasant's dress he had worn in the morning, and there to put his answer into the hands of a labouring clod in the gardens. This he did, begging him to take "Mr. Davis tailior's acquoint for the French lady, up speedy to the house."

The obliging clod complied, and Leslie returned to his lodging, and early in the evening to the woods, expecting the guileless creature who put such confidence in him. Nor was he disappointed. About nine o'clock, of a warm, moonlit, September evening, Leslie standing anxiously in the wood-path, saw Elinor coming along it to meet him.

"How good you are," she said, as they met; "but indeed I did not mean to trouble you thus. I thought you would have written to me; indeed, I did not think of your coming."

"But you are not displeased?" said Leslie, taking her hand, which she withdrew when she had performed the proper greeting. "For my part, I am so happy to be of any service to you, I am so happy to see you again, that I cannot but bless the difficulties which have brought this meeting about."

"Oh! Mr. Leslie, I am sure you would not say so, if you knew how miserable I have been."

"But you are miserable no longer, are you?" said Leslie; "you feel that I am able and willing to remove every cause of pain—I am able to make you happy."

"I hope so," said Elinor; "but it will be a long time before I can pay you."

"What! pay me? Oh! I was not thinking of that; I was thinking," said Leslie, drawing her gently to the fallen tree, where he had watched her sitting those autumn days, and placing himself beside her—"I was thinking whether you did not know that I look upon this moment, when you trust me, when I you apply to me, when you know me to be a better friend than any of those whom chance has thrown you amongst, as the most delightful that ever in all my youth and enjoyment passed over me"—he possessed himself of her hand—"and I don't deceive myself, do I? You know me to be your truest well-wisher, your most anxious counsellor, the person who would desire your happiness beyond all other things, and do whatever may best promote it."

Elinor's hand stayed in his, but it was with the calmest voice she answered, "Yes, or you would not be here to help me."

"No, no! and you felt it was none of those guardians of yours, who was willing to do so?—you did not apply to them?"

"Oh! I should never have done such a thing," said Elinor, the slightest smile passing over her face, as at the suggestion of something wholly out of the question.

"I have a kind of right, you have given me a right to counsel you, guard you; you are inclined to do as I advise you?"

"Yes," said Elinor, with a mournful inflection in her voice. "I know nothing at all of this world I am in, and I have found you wise, knowing everything. You can teach me what you please, but I know you will teach me what is right."

"Ah, yes! right—the right way to be happy—and we are creatures made to be happy, not to suffer pain from each, other, not to be unkindly treated, but to seek out those who love us, and to put all our trust that what they do will be the best they know how to do, for our happiness."

Elinor was silent. She was listening, and trying to comprehend.

"Elinor, did any ever devote themselves to you, and think, of nothing except how to please, how to take care of you; what you liked, where you would go?"

"Oh! no, certainly," said Elinor.

"Your kind Mother in the Convent, your teachers the nuns, your companions—did you ever feel that when you came they rejoiced, when you went they mourned; that you were the thing they first thought of at waking; the object for which they planned their plans, lamented their failures?"

"No!" said Elinor, "they were not so unreasonable."

"But he who loves you is so unreasonable, so reasonable at the same time, for that which is dearer than oneself must be more present, more cherished than oneself—the happiness of that creature must be before every other wish and plan. Would it be no pleasure, dearest Elinor, to be thus beloved?"

His right hand suddenly transferred her's to his left, and went round her waist, nor did it fail to press that slender, warm column, which it had encircled. Elinor did not withdraw, but she raised her clear eyes to his, and met his fierce glance with such inquiring, innocent calmness, that his arm released its hold, and he did but raise her hand to his mouth, and pressed one kiss upon it.

"May I not love you, Elinor?"

"Indeed I think you do," said Elinor.

"I doubt whether you do as much for me," said Leslie, to himself, and he felt that he should but set her on her guard by any further revelation of his feelings; but he was not wholly displeased with the step he had advanced. All recollection of the cause of their meeting had departed from him; but while he was thinking how best to go on with the interview, Elinor took advantage of the pause, and returned to the difficulties he was to settle for her, which to him appeared prosaic and superfluous, but to her was the thing that made their meeting interesting. Leslie took from her hand the little neat bundle of papers which she produced; he comprehended that Laura had not chosen to explain or soften anything, and promised that he would himself arrange all.

He would then have passed to other subjects, but Elinor would stay no longer after she had fulfilled her errand, and then he fixed the next afternoon for another meeting at the same place, to give account of what he should have done.

"Say nothing of our meeting," said he; "it is best not. I can scarcely explain why; but promise that you will follow my advice."

Elinor did so. She had no conscience but Leslie—her own had never come much into activity, and that which she brought from the Convent had been all overthrown.

Elinor returned to the house, and to the saloon where Mr. Chanson and his sister Laura were sitting, and entering it with her light, noiseless movement, was taking up her work, and about to seat herself in her usual place, when Laura stopped her, by asking, in a constrained voice,

"Where have you been, Elinor?"

"In the wood," said Elinor, the colour rising, she knew not why.

"But, my dear," said the Squire, "that's not the proper place for a young girl like you, at night, all alone; you should not go there."

"And were you alone?" said Laura, briefly.

Elinor had nothing to say; the question was so home, that it admitted but of yes or no; one of which she might not, and the other she would not say.

"Speak out," said Mr. Chanson; "don't be afraid of us. Tell the truth always."

"Oh, yes! that I will, always," said Elinor.

"You were alone, then, I dare say, were you not?" said Mr. Chanson. "Still I don't like you to wander about alone, and you will do it no more, will you?"

"Very well," said Elinor.

But Laura, speaking almost at the same time, said, "You were not alone, then; you can't deny it, Elinor. You went there to meet somebody."

Elinor answered nothing, but bent her head over her sewing, and had the tears in her eyes.

Mr. Chanson was almost as much embarrassed as she. He rose up, crushed the newspaper, and turning his back, leaned on the mantel-shelf, taking part in his own heat heeat with the embarrassed young girl, against his sister, though the latter was clearly in the right.

"Was it Mr. Leslie?" said Laura.

"Oh! Mr. Leslie!" said her brother, half turning round; "quite impossible."

Laura could not be quite sure it was he, for though, indeed, the broken seal of Elinor's letter had revealed the intercourse between them, she could not comprehend by what means he could so rapidly have obeyed the summons; yet she could not but feel it must be Leslie, and her anxiety and dread about it were extreme.

"Speak, Elinor! say whether or not it was he."

"No, no," said Mr. Chanson; "there is no sense in asking such a thing. I had a letter from him two days ago, about the distemper-powders; he was not going from home—besides ......"

What there was besides he did not explain, but Elinor took courage under this unexpected defence, and though she would not say a word of denial herself, felt half justified by the denial he extemporised, and sewed away, supported in the silence she resolved to observe. Laura, on the other hand, was unduly discouraged, and her pressing investigation, which must have ended in a victory, resulted in an impatient "Well!" and the three sat in the most uncomfortable silence, till Elinor, who felt thoroughly humble, and anxious to do something right, though she could not do the one right thing they wanted, so anxiously watched her chances of finding the Squire's spectacles, picking up his book, and placing it softly on the table when it fell out of his slumbering hand, of remembering where Laura had laid down the key of the tea-chest, of letting Puff out of the room, and letting him in again, that Mr. Chanson's heart was quite softened, and gently touching her head, he said, in a low voice,

"You are a good little girl—only mind what Laura tells you;" and Elinor was so pleased with the kind words, that she felt as if she should never obey anybody else, nor perhaps would she, had there been as much womanly kindness and sincerity in the sister as of gentleness in the brother.

But Laura had feelings quite apart from the interests of Elinor, which prevented any approach to kindliness, and those were her own concern in Leslie, and in all that he did. He had secured a place in her affections such as he never aspired to, and which, at this time, he would much rather have been without; and it made Laura wild with jealousy to think that one day Elinor might occupy the place which she herself, with all her beauty, wit, and wealth, longed for in vain. Should those two be coming and going together, civil to her, but lovers of each other? should it be by short and transient fits that she should see Leslie, but Elinor be of his house, always his and with him? should the stranger's sustained attention be for her, but the word, the sign, the look, the understood gesture, be for Elinor? Laura could not endure it, and the thing was so inadmissible, that whatever she could do to prevent it seemed the thing to be done—not the right thing, perhaps, but still to be done. She hated Elinor, and would willingly have seen in her all those defects which would disenchant Leslie; she wished they were in her, and acknowledged to be there by everybody; and when Elinor had gently crept out of the room, at an early bedtime, she broke the long silence that had descended upon them all, and began to talk in an ingenuous, candid tone, to her brother.

"There are great excuses to be made for that poor child," said she. "The liberty she enjoys is so sudden, and the training she has had is so bad, that she is liable to errors from which other people are free."

"Yes, indeed," said the Squire; "and it is very kind and just of you, Laura, to make excuses for her. She wants a friend."

"Yes! I only wish she were more willing to listen to me."

"She is a little wilful, is she?"

"I think you must have perceived that. " Don't you see how she keeps apart all the morning? I am always willing—anxious—that she should come to my room and be with me; but was not it strange, how she persecuted Mr. Leslie to attend to her?—not unnatural certainly—a man was a marvel to a girl from a convent; but I explained to her the common forms of society, and she should have altered her conduct in consequence; however, it was just the same, and I'm afraid, I really am, that this walk of hers has something to do with an appointment—if not with him, with somebody else."

"I hope not," said the Squire; "though, indeed, I saw that Leslie was rather in love with her."

"Oh! no, no!" cried Laura, anxiously; "a man is always flattered if a girl shows any liking for him, but that's all. How could he take a fancy for a child like that—uneducated yet artificial, not pretty nor amusing?"

"She does not say much," answered the Squire.

"Besides, Lawrence," went on Miss Chanson, "though he might have been pleased with her, if he had been wholly fancy-free, yet—being as he is ......"

"What? is Leslie in love with anybody—hey; Laura! is that it? is it possible, my dear?"

"I have never said a word to any human being before," said Laura, turning away her head.

"Is it possible? The thing I should like beyond all others; why did not I know?"

"Nay, you think more of it than you ought. Indeed, Lawrence, I don't quite understand him; something. is on his mind, which—which ...... in short, there has no word passed between us. Has he any fortune? Sometimes I have thought, that knowing me to have a large one, his own want of any may have held him back."

"Oh! he is not poor, but very proud. Are you civil enough to him, Laura?"

"Nay, certainly," said Laura; "it is for him to seek, not me."

"Yes, yes; but at the same time, I can tell you that Fanny Wimbledon would have been Mrs. Chanson, if she had not thought it necessary to chaff and flout me, when I was looking for a kind word."

"Did she like you, vain man?".

"So I heard afterwards; but I was in Caithness, and it was too far to come back. So don't throw him away—that is, if you think you could like him."

"Lawrence, you are mother and brother to me;" and she laid her head on his shoulder. "I do like him."

"Is it so, dear Laura?" said he, fondly caressing her; "then may Providence bring you and him together. If I can help you …."

"Only say nothing to him. Oh! for heaven's sake! do nothing rash. Proud he is, and a word might alarm him. But it is a comfort, brother, to have made a confidant of you, and to you I am not ashamed of saying what no mortal ear besides must know."

Thus talked brother and sister; it was a pity that Laura knew all the time that she was lying. Those words of her own, "I have never revealed it to another human being," took herself in, for although they conveyed a great deal, they affirmed nothing.

Elinor was perplexed beyond measure what to do about her next day's engagement. The utmost she wished was to tell Leslie that she could meet him no more; but she knew not by what means to effect this. Laura would not let her go beyond her sight. The room, which she had declared herself so anxious should be common between them, was for the first time opened to Elinor; she took a pretext of some fine lace, which was in bad condition, and which Elinor, profiting by a convent accomplishment, had once offered to put in order. She had then told how a certain veil had been wanted for an image of the Virgin, in a procession, and how it had been trusted to her to put to rights, when some others had refused through fear of its tenderness. She had spread it on a thick bed of cambric, and then, by patient immersions in certain prepared waters, had removed every trace of dirt and stain, without the least violence to the frail fabric, so that when the image appeared in it next day, inquiries had been made who could so successfully have renovated the delicate fabric.

This had been a tale of the early days of her arrival, and she was surprised to-day at Laura's recollection of it, and not best pleased that the occupation should have been given her just this morning. Then followed a drive in which Elinor was included, the object of which was to meet a young relation of the Chansons, Sir Peter Bicester, who had just got orders to join his regiment in Ceylon, and was coming for a farewell visit to Chanson Wood. He was a lively, thoughtless lad of eighteen, a great admirer of his cousin Laura, who was six years older than he, and in his intense attentions, during their after-dinner saunter in the garden, Laura lost sight of Elinor, and Elinor, with the speed of an Italian greyhound, ran to the waterfall to say one word, and but one, to Leslie. In case of not finding him, she had provided herself with a little note, merely, "I cannot come this evening. Mr. Chanson forbids me to go out.— ELINOR LADYLIFT." This she intended to lay on the fallen tree, and trusted it would be found by Leslie, should she not meet with him.

Leslie had been there early—as early as he thought it possible the usual morning ride or drive of the others would set Elinor at liberty—and the longer she delayed, the stronger the fear became that he should not see her, so much the intenser grew his desire to do so, and the regard in which he held the object of it.

"Innocent and artless Elinor!" thought he; "with a whole heart to give, a whole nature to be made happy, is there anything better in life than to make and share your happiness?" and then more dreamily his thoughts dwelt upon images of virtuous felicity, upon the meanness of betraying such guileless confidence, and upon the difficulty which he had not hitherto counted upon of converting her quiet feeling into one of passion.

It was already quite dusk, when his ear at last caught a footfall. It was of one running quickly; and eagerly springing to meet her, he at last beheld Elinor, and felt an almost unknown pleasure in the reality that she was there.

"I am here for one minute only," said she. "Mr. Chanson forbade me to walk out in the evening. I only wanted to tell you not to wait."

"And why?" said Leslie, holding fast her hand.

"He says it is wrong. You did not tell me so, or I would not have done it."

"I know no wrong; but you must not go yet. What! will you not stay to know what I have been doing for you? All is settled now."

"Oh! kind friend," said Elinor, receiving the little bundle of papers which he had prepared so as to look business-like (taking care that in fact they should trouble her no more), "how can I thank you? I can only say thank you—thank you—Mr. Leslie, good—good Mr. Leslie. Farewell! I must not stay; let me go."

"And it is this moment I have been waiting for all day," said he.

"Have you, indeed? I am very sorry to have kept you so long. How kind of you not to have gone away. But I am so glad you did stay; I had got a note written for you, but I should have been uncertain whether you received it."

"A note!" cried Leslie; "let me have it;" and perceiving it closed in her hand, he gently took that hand, to draw the paper from when a violent start from Elinor made him, too, start, and looking where she looked, he saw Laura standing but a few yards from them. She came forward directly that she perceived she was observed.

"Elinor," said she, "is it thus you keep your promise?"

"I did not promise," said Elinor; "besides, I came only to say that I could not come."

"Go home," said Laura, in a low, trembling voice.

Leslie did not mean to be scolded like a schoolboy; he approached Elinor with the open, commonplace air of an acquaintance, and offering his hand, "Good evening, then, Miss Ladylift," said he. "It gives me great pleasure if I have been useful to you, and I trust you will command my services on any future occasion."

"Go home, Elinor," Miss Chanson repeated, and Elinor, puzzled, moved away and disappeared, letting fall, as she did so, the little twisted note, which by this time she had forgotten.

Laura, meantime, made several efforts to speak, while Leslie politely waited, his eyes averted, and only listening indifferently for anything she might wish to say. But he was surprised and startled out of this indifference by a sudden outburst of tears from Laura, who, unable to withhold her emotion any longer, gave way, and wept like one most miserable.

"Miss Chanson," said he, coming up to her; "alas! what is the matter? Are you ill? can I do anything? Lean on me, I beseech you."

Laura's tears flowed only the more profusely, and it was in vain she used her utmost effort to restrain the sobs which burst from her breast. She did, in fact, put her hand on his arm, but she turned away her head, and avoided, as much as she could, any support or assistance he would have given her.

"Forgive me. I did not know I was so weak. I am ashamed, like one on the rack. Pain and shame—pain and shame for me who have been so proud, so sheltered from both!"

"What is it you mean?" cried Leslie, feeling the awkwardness of his position, yet not displeased at its novelty, only quite resolved to commit himself in no manner, and to no thing. "Why, or how, can Miss Chanson be the subject of pain?"

"I shall not be, if I can think I am your sister," said she, suddenly. "A sister prefers her brother's happiness to her own—if he is happy, so is she. I have just learned what are your feelings. I did not always know them, but I do now ......"

Her voice broke off, and though she tried to go on she could not.

"What do you know?" said Leslie, not at all choosing that Laura should force herself on him as a confidant, nor be able to say that he was the lover of Elinor. "I have nothing to discover, beyond a casual circumstance in which I have been of some slight use to your friend, but if it is true I am to hope for the kindness of a sister here"—and he tried to take her hand, which she very hastily snatched away—" my happiness would be great in proportion to my want since infancy, of every kindly home tie."

Laura raised her large, fine eyes to his, with a look interpreted by him to mean, "Is that indeed all you can feel?" and then suddenly put out her hand, which he took, and felt that it trembled.

"Be it so! yes," said Laura, "and now believe that I will promote your wishes in any way you will direct me. I have no self any longer."

"How can I thank you," said Leslie; "but do not mistake me—I want no service from any one. I have no wishes, unless, indeed, I might entertain that of again enjoying the pleasure of such society as made my life happy under your roof."

Laura sighed deeply, and shook her head. "Ah, yes! you use such words very lightly. Well, be it so; come to us again, Mr. Leslie, and if ...... am I not your sister?" she concluded, at last, in an eager, abrupt voice.

"I feel," said Leslie—not knowing what to say he felt—" I, the most unworthy ......"

"I'll explain that I met you," said Laura, breaking off what he was saying very impatiently; "you will be very welcome to my brother—my real brother," she added, forcing a smile to her pale lips. "To-morrow, then," and she moved away; but in all her violence of emotion, she had recollected the little twisted note, and had stooped and secured it, without attracting Leslie's attention to it.

"What is all this?" thought Leslie, looking after her as she hastily disappeared. "I am to understand that she thought me her lover! and not only forgiven, but taken for a brother. Brother, indeed! There's something generous about her—romantic enough. But how unlike Elinor—that inquiring, innocent look, those confiding eyes! Why should this Laura want me to see more of her? Can it be real generosity? But I will have nobody force upon me the character of a lover. I am free!"

CHAPTER VI

Laura had now entered on a desperate game, which she resolved at every hazard should end in making her the wife of Leslie. Right is so much the essential point in our actions, that scarce any villany is deliberately done without justifying it to ourselves; and so Laura, when not abandoned to passion, found good reasons in the advantages to Leslie, and in her own superior powers of making him happy, to carry her along the path from which she could not think of turning. Every instrument must be laid hold of; she had already made her brother an unconscious volunteer, and she next prepared her cousin to assist in the cause.

The same fiction which had served with Mr. Chanson she made use of to Sir Peter. His flame for Laura was not such as to make him stand in the way of any serious matrimonial project; on the contrary, he would have been proud to see her chosen by some cavalier of high merit, an alliance with whom would have made everything splendid and jovial, and creditable to his own admiration. That his cousin Laura should be neglected, or laid aside for another, was as impossible as it would be humiliating; and Laura, who had a good insight into motives and character, availed herself of this feeling. She had only to sigh a little, and cast her eyes once or twice to the ceiling, before Sir Peter inquired whether anything on earth, that he could affect, had vexed his darling Laura; and then, with a graceful show of candour, and of that confidence which a woman may show to a boy, but a boy already worth trusting, did Laura partly hint, and partly tell the same lie she had told her brother, and which she was beginning to believe herself.

Sir Peter's indignation was boundless—his desire to approve himself her true knight zealous—he would fight Leslie to-day if she pleased. Laura had only to temper his ardour, and to insinuate that at the, point matters were arrived at between herself and Leslie, anything which injured him, or drove him into a shyness of the family, would be fatal to her interests. No, the only thing Sir Peter could do, was to occupy Elinor's attention. a little, keep her from such "open flirtation" with Leslie.

"There is no harm in that, is there Pet—is there Peter?"

"I should think not, indeed—little coquette that she is—and fool that he is, not to see through such feminine arts. She a nun, indeed!"

Accordingly, the day when Leslie thought proper to accept the invitation forwarded by Mr. Chanson, upon hearing from his sister that she had accidentally met him, Sir Peter went up to Elinor the moment she came into the drawing-room, and forced her into talk, which he continued as he took her into dinner, and sat himself down beside her. Leslie had given his arm to Laura, as mistress of the house, and had quite determined to pay no attention to Elinor, such as could justify Laura in "talking secrets" with him; but he was not prepared to see Elinor an object of attention to another; and apparently well pleased to be so.

And so, in fact, she was, for her whole being was at ease now that Leslie was returned, and she had leisure to listen to her companion, who was as young as herself, and very gay and droll, and made her laugh, as girls will at nonsense. Leslie had habits of perfect self-control, though he was so young, and he forced himself to be at ease so successfully, that Laura could not determine in her own mind whether he observed what was going on or not. Careless as he seemed, however, he was watching them, and a jealous pang shot through Leslie's heart, as to whether it was possible that this young soldier should ever have indeed had an opportunity of seeing Elinor as he had done in that deep wood, by that fair fall of waters; and though his consciousness said no, still the question made him watch uneasily the progress of their intercourse.

After dinner, Sir Peter, intent on the interests of his cousin, still kept up the attempt to monopolise Elinor. He had provided for so doing by engaging her beforehand to sing a particular song for him, which, by a great effort of his memory; he had succeeded in remembering to have heard from her the evening of his arrival, and when the party was settling to the employments of the evening, he followed Laura to the piano-forte, near which Elinor was working, and while Laura played, began to request the execution of the promise he had obtained.

"If you like," said Elinor, "by and by; but will you be so kind as to let me sing later? Miss Chanson wishes those ladies to sing, she told me."

Sir Peter could not but comply with this modest request, so unlike the answer of young ladies more in the world, and moved away, while Leslie abruptly took his place, sitting down beside her, and assuming that he had that right to her attention which a secret between them brought with it.

"You are happy now, are you not?" said he; "there are no more such tears as you say you shed over that little bundle of papers?"

Elinor looked up, frightened lest any one should hear.

"No one is listening to us," said Leslie, "no one can tell what we are saying; the insufferable drumming of the piano-forte prevents the human voice from being heard."

"Drumming!" said Elinor, with a sudden smile of surprise; "nay, is it not very good playing?"

"Do you like it?" said Leslie, suddenly.

"Oh, yes! it is very good indeed."

"Do you like it?" repeated Leslie, smiling also, but urging his question.

"I think so," said Elinor; "one ought to like what other people are so kind as to do, and it is very difficult music."

"Still you do not answer. Do you like that loud, hard drumming?"

"When you say loud and hard," said Elinor, "you teach me what to say. Nobody likes what they can call loud, hard drumming."

"I prejudice you! That is very true," said Leslie. "So we will leave off talking about it, and I will entreat you, the moment it is over, to replace it, by singing the Spirit Song. Do you remember, you studied it for me?"

"Yes; and since you have been away I have studied it more, and can sing it better," said Elinor.

"Who would do that for me, except yourself?" said Leslie. "Nobody cares where I go, or what I like, or when I shall be back, or whether I die on the road, or live."

"I do," said Elinor; "and people who know you better must care more than I."

"If you say so, never mind the rest of the world," said Leslie; "and now the piano-forte is at rest. Come, dear Miss Ladylift, let me hear my song."

Elinor rose, but hung back, while Leslie obtained Laura's permission. Laura assented.

"Nay, why do you ask me? I am always delighted when Elinor can be persuaded to let us hear that lovely voice. I merely played a little air to bring people round the piano-forte." And while she spoke, she looked round for her cousin, and summoned him by a glance, which he well understood, and rushed to the rescue, seeing which, Laura moved away, and left the coming skirmish to do what mischief it would.

"I am so glad to see you ready to sing," said Sir Peter; "I was afraid I should have to wait long for Adeste."

"Miss Ladylift is going to have the kindness to sing a song which I have begged for," said Leslie, stiffly.

"But mine first, I hope; you promised me first," said Sir Peter, in the blandest tone.

"I think you had the goodness to get up on purpose to oblige me," said Leslie, "did not you?"

"Yes," said Elinor, frightened, and looking round for Laura.

"Then let me find it; here's the book I know—yes, here is the song."

"Ah! that's not fair," said Sir Peter, "you don't forget how very kindly you granted my petition, and I have been depending upon you."

"I did promise him," said Elinor, looking at Leslie humbly and appealingly.

"Did you," said Leslie, very coldly; "nay, don't allow me to interfere with your arrangements."

"I can't be so indifferent," said Sir Peter; "mine, mine first; Mr. Leslie, you see, says it does not matter."

"Allow Miss Ladylift to determine that point," said Leslie.

"May I?" said Elinor, joyfully, thinking if she might settle it, the difficulty was over; "then let me sing first Adeste, and yours afterwards, Mr. Leslie."

Leslie made no answer, except a bow, and stepping backward, withdrew from the circle round the piano-forte; nor returned to claim the song which Elinor, when she had got through Sir Peter's, at once looked round for him to hear. Her sham admirer did all in his power to take her attention from the real one, but Elinor could by no means regain the composure Leslie's displeasure had taken from her, and she sought with her timid eyes, all the evening, the opportunity of obtaining reconciliation, which he steadily withheld.

Thus ended the first day of the visit, to which she had looked forward as the time of such happiness.

Laura next morning took her to task.

"What makes you walk about with such a mournful air?" said she; "you look like a naughty child who wants to kiss and make it up. What ails you?"

"I am not a child," said Elinor, in her sweet, humble voice; "but I am what you please to call naughty ......"

"And want to kiss?" said Laura, scornfully.

"No," said Elinor, hurt at being turned into ridicule, and at receiving reproof in a spirit that did not deserve that treatment.

"What then," said Laura, "and who is it you have offended?"

"I am afraid I have offended Mr. Leslie."

"Is it possible you think enough of a man of his age, indeed any age, to trouble yourself about offending him or not?" said Laura.

"Why should not I?" said Elinor, aghast.

"Because," answered Laura, breaking out; "it is the most absurd thing for a girl with any proper spirit, I ever heard of in my life."

"But I have no proper spirit," said Elinor, who felt that if Leslie would forgive her, she would beg pardon from him with all her heart.

"You don't know even what it is," said Laura; "upon my word, your conduct is perfectly indelicate. You might almost as well go and ask him if he will be kind enough to accept you for his wife."

"His wife!" cried Elinor, quickly; "what has that to do with being sorry to have displeased him? Wife! what can you mean?"

"Nonsense! I do hate affected innocence, and all that stuff, merely to impose upon a man. Heaven knows they are open enough to flattery; but, really you must allow me to say, that you persecute Mr. Leslie, with yours. You follow him about, and look at him, and invite him to your side, and force him, really force him to pay you attentions, which he probably would willingly he paying elsewhere, only he can't get rid of you."

"Oh! indeed, indeed, you mistake!" said Elinor, almost amazed to death; "he can get rid of me any moment. Think how he went away yesterday evening, and would not even say good night, and indeed I am afraid to seem to be intrusive, and I never do put myself in his way, or do anything to speak to him, unless it comes naturally from him."

"You mean, in short," said Laura, most disdainfully, "that his constant attendance proceeds solely from his own wish for your society."

"Yes, I suppose so," said Elinor, bewildered; "I don't know any other reason."

"Really, you are a perfect simpleton, or choose to seem so," said Laura.

"I dare say he is sorry for me," said Elinor, seeking excuses for Leslie's kindness. "I am away from all my friends, and he is very, very kind in giving me advice."

"And what right have you to ask him, rather than me," said Laura; "most women like to consult women, rather than young men, and most people will judge those who do otherwise, to be as forward and as bold, as I must say, Elinor, you seem to me."

"Am I bold?" said Elinor, sadly, feeling so fearful, and so shy, that she could not comprehend the reproach, and as Laura was habitually out of temper with her, taking it as an instance of what she must meekly bear from her hostess, rather than as a true accusation against herself.

It influenced her conduct however, towards Leslie, for under Laura's eye she could not act with the total unconsciousness of her behaviour hitherto; she was obliged to act by rule, for she had no feeling of having transgressed a woman's duty, and therefore no impulse to direct her. There was, however, always such quiet maidenliness about her, that it was only by a shade that she was altered, and Leslie being on his high horse, did not so much as perceive it, but thought all the reserve, and all the withdrawal of friendliness was on his own side.

Sir Peter learned through Laura, that his plot had succeeded, and took a boyish delight in the mischief made, over which he laughed with his cousin, as two children do over a ringdove in a string, which they are tormenting; but Elinor, if she did not offer apologies to her kind friend Leslie, had no spirit or inclination to laugh or talk with Sir Peter, and was almost as silent to him as she had been to Leslie, the first time he sat by her at breakfast.

In this mood, the amusements of the day were arranged. Men have a way of employing themselves at amusements, which causes their feelings to become secondary to their sports, and thus Leslie, angry, even anxious as he was, yet took it as a matter of course that he should join heart and soul in the pastime suggested by Sir Peter, and accepted by the Squire. This was a drag, which an adept sportsman was quickly sent forward to lead over the country, choosing puzzling places, and paths difficult to follow, in order to try the power of some young blood hounds belonging to Mr. Chanson. The most perplexing pass thus selected, was a profound gap in the country, at the bottom of which ran the brook which formed the waterfall in the wood; and the rocky sides of which fringed with trees and bushes, rose very far above the bed of the stream.

On one side of this, Laura promised to take her station, and Elinor was to accompany her in order to witness the achievements of the hounds in these difficult circumstances. There is no faster running than a drag, and luckily for the sportsmen, the day was a cool one, of the now declining autumn, and the slight frost made the scent puzzling enough to try the acumen of the eager hounds. They had a long circuit to make before they should reach the final point where the ladies were to await them, and these latter had arrived at the rendezvous some time before any sound of the chase broke upon the amber stillness of the autumn scene.

They sat down together on the stump of a tree, Laura holding a book, and Elinor producing from the pocket of her black apron a bit of curiously fine cambric, on which she was working a cobweb pattern, the whole of which could have been rolled into a walnut shell. They were quite silent. Elinor was afraid of Laura, and her spirits froze under the unsympathetic influence. To-day, especially she was shut into herself, and she mechanically pursued the occupation before her, so far pleased that Laura did not disturb her in it.

At length the cheerfulest of sounds broke the silence, the distant tongue of hounds, rising and falling, bursting out and subsiding. It was a natural piano and forte exactly suiting woods and dingles, and inspiring the ear, which heard them for the first time, with the delight of an unexplored pleasure. Elinor, finely strung to sounds, took in these with a curiosity and enjoyment which made her fingers stay on her work, and her heart send a flush of blood into her changeful cheeks.

"Are they coming?" she said, at last, half rising, and looking at her companion.

"It seems so," said Laura, coldly, rising also; "I suppose you can hear the hounds?"

"Yes, and now they are nearer; they seem going away again; there! do listen, there's an echo."

"Everybody knows that," said Laura.

She walked forward, and Elinor by her side, they approached very nearly the rocky gap worn by the water; they could hear the boom of the waterfall far below and the unaccountable changefulness in the intensity of its sound which running water gives out. It was a wide gap, and presently the bay of the hounds increasing, they saw white spots glancing among the underwood, then the whole shape and colour of the hounds, full of the tension of the pursuit, and puzzling out their way to the brink of the chasm. Here the foremost threw up his head, and changed his note to one of distress; others came up, scented the prey to the very edge, and then ceasing their cry of pursuit, seemed measuring the leap, and with distracted anxiety ran to and fro, tempting themselves to pass it.

At this moment a horseman arrived; he alighted, and cheered the hounds to persevere. It was Mr. Chanson himself; he knew the secret pass intended for them, but would only act like magical music, applauding their better guesses, but not explaining wherein the achievement lay. They were maddened to accomplish it, by his voice, and at last the hound which first came up put himself over the edge, where there seemed no hold, and whimpering at what he was about to venture, passed down the rock a little way, seemed to find a point where the leap was possible, and presently breaking out into music again, was seen emerging almost perpendicularly on the other side of the chasm, and away in full cry on the opposite bank. Once taught the way, the others followed, and Mr. Chanson as soon as he saw they were over, turned his horse up the stream, and gallopped away to a further point where was a bridge. He met Sir Peter as he went, and turned him on the same path as himself; a minute afterwards the third horseman came up, Leslie, making straight to the chasm. His horse and he had been down, as appeared by the mud they were covered with, and to make up for the time they had lost, were going their best pace on the track the rider judged by the sound, would bring him straight to the hounds.

As he neared the chasm, he caught a glance of the horsemen who were now on the other side; he checked the speed of his horse a little, encouraged him by his voice and hand, and then rode steadily towards the leap. Laura, aware of the danger, cried to him to turn up the stream, but though he saw the difficulty, and though he had no wish to be killed, he was at the age, when it seems a matter of course not to be killed, and not to fail; and disregarding her entreaties, put his horse at the leap, and got safe over. Laura as pale as a corpse, shrieked loudly as he leaped. Elinor, quite ignorant there was any peril, was excited by the stirring sight, so that she clapped her hands, laughed, and leaped with delight. Leslie saw them both, and when the impetus following the leap slackened, he stopped his horse, and giving up the pursuit turned him, and dismounted beside the ladies.

"They have run into it now," said he; "I may as well stop at once."

Laura had been so thoroughly frightened, that she did not instantly recover. She remonstrated with him on the rashness with genuine emotion, which he easily distinguished from any affected nervousness, and was flattered by it; but it amused him much more to see Elinor's excited look, which turned to perplexity, as she heard and saw Laura's alarm.

"My horse did it gallantly, did not he?" said Leslie, looking cheerily at Elinor, whose face caught and returned his smile.

"Like flying," said Elinor; "it was very pretty."

"How childish you are!" said Laura; "you know nothing of the danger."

"After all, there was none," said Leslie, "and the appearance of it gave zest to the leap."

"It is very pleasant," said Elinor, "to see danger, if one is safe."

"How do you know that?" said Leslie.

"Because in the convent," said Elinor; answering quickly to his quick question, "the waves used to dash against the garden wall, but could not come in, and we all liked to be near them. But once the waves broke over, and then we all ran away."

Leslie laughed, and looked investigatingly at Elinor's face which had blushed brightly, as she replied to his imperative question, and he was thinking why she blushed. Laura was little pleased at this effect of Elinor's simplicity, and seeing him inclined to turn his attention entirely to her young companion, suddenly declared herself tired, and said they would go home. She chose a path along the rocky channel of the brook, where no horse could be even led, and could not refrain from turning her shoulder pettishly to Leslie as they parted. He scarcely observed it, he had forgotten also his reigned anger with Elinor, and he rode gently away, thinking of the little scene that had passed.

"How moveable her nature is," said he. "It was made on purpose, I think, to complete mine, cast in my mould, when a man had been completed, and it was fit only to form a woman."

CHAPTER VII

Elinor accepted peace with Leslie gladly and gratefully. Nothing was said between them, but they resumed without words their former position. He did not want—from her at least—any show of spirit, or assertion of the rights of woman; the meek glad cordiality of the young gift was what enchanted him.

"I should have taken Leslie for Elinor's lover, if you had not told me, Laura," said her brother.

The word went like a dagger through her heart, but she smiled as though the thing were beneath notice, and said merely, "Oh! that little girl! he is good natured to her." And Mr. Chanson was willing to adopt her view of the subject. Nevertheless he would have been glad the expected word should have been said, which plighted his guest and his sister; and one morning as they stood together, after breakfast, in front of a great dahlia bed, he broke out into words.

"This is all my sister's doing, the whole of this garden; I know nothing of such matters, and it is very lucky for me to have a woman of so much taste and manner at the head of my establishment."

Leslie had been profoundly meditating on Elinor, but roused himself to answer. "Indeed it is; we are glad enough of the result, but we don't like the trouble of providing for it beforehand."

"Laura is uncommonly clever about the management of one's house," said her brother, "indeed about everything. She looks well, don't she, at the head of one's table? I am proud of her."

"With great reasons," said Leslie.

Mr. Chanson was warmed by this agreement.

"And it is my good luck that a girl who might have her own house in London, and do what she likes—for she has all her mother's property—she is only my half sister, you know, and her mother had Kitsal, you know, at her brother's death."

"Kitsal," said Leslie, absently, but with a kind of wise voice, as though that word explained the whole matter.

"It was turned into money," said the Squire. "If Laura should ever marry, I should try to keep her interested in the county by giving my influence to bring her husband into Parliament; I could do it, sir. They want a Whig, and at the next election, I could, and I would do it."

"That's an object worth every man's ambition," said Leslie. "I wonder you never put yourself in, you would surely have liked it."

"No, no, it's not the place for me; I was young once, but I never could hear anybody talk above ten minutes without falling asleep, and what should I do therefore in the House of Commons? I leave all that to the clever men and the fine gentlemen. It is not in me."

Mr. Chanson was pleased with himself for this successful exposition of the advantages which an alliance with Laura held out, and when he saw Leslie in the course of the day talking with his sister, he repeated to himself with inward self applause "it works, it works!"

Sir Peter also tried to put in a good word for her; "Desperately fine shoulders my cousin has," said he, looking at her in a becoming evening dress; "she is a fine creature, don't you think so, yourself?"

"To be sure, everybody must; good colouring too—bright and clear."

"Yes, very unlike that little pale sparrow," said Sir Peter, designating Elinor.

"Sparrow! oh yes! she chirps nicely, don't you think so, yourself?" said Leslie.

"What her singing? I am not very learned about music, but I was much indebted to her for obliging me so about that song the other night."

Nobody ever caught Leslie wincing under a sudden attack, he answered readily. "Ay, she was conscientious in keeping her first engagement."

Sir Peter laughed; "I doubt," said he, "whether that would be uppermost in her thoughts. Conventual as she has been, she has no objection to learn the polite art of flirtation; you see that yourself?"

"Not I," said Leslie, "I've something else to do; and I apprehend if I had not, that little sparrow would only chirp defiance at me."

"I apprehend no such thing," said Sir Peter, "I mean to have a walk and a talk with her to-morrow morning; just keep my secret, and don't spoil sport."

"It is no matter of mine," said Leslie.

"You have other views, perhaps," said Sir Peter.

"What?" said Leslie, in a quite altered tone, which sounded very much like, "Don't be impertinent."

But Elinor! Leslie felt she did not love him, that her regard was one of respect and liking, such as she felt for the old Holy Mother in the convent, only tempered by the unholiness of his sex and conversation, and he did not know but what the giddy and prattling Sir Peter might succeed in inspiring those feelings of which she was hitherto ignorant. But he could have no intentions except those of amusing himself for the hour, and Leslie felt quite indignant that any man except himself, should entertain views which could interfere with her happiness. He resolved to warn her; and at dinner when a large party were all talking, he asked her what were her engagements for the next day. Elinor did not know that she had any.

"I said I would show Sir Peter where the stones with shells in them are to be found," she added, after a pause.

"Why did you say you had no engagement, then?" said Leslie, abruptly.

His tone made her blush suddenly, for it alarmed her with the feeling of having unconsciously said what she ought not; but after two or three seconds she answered, "because I forgot it."

Leslie did not believe her, he saw the rising blood, and interpreted it his own way; but the one truth told about her intended walk was enough effort, without requiring a second about her motive, and he went on, "Don't do as you promised."

"No?" said Elinor, astonished.

"Let older people show him the stones with shells in them," said he, "you had better not."

"Why?" asked Elinor, "I once showed them to you."

"Yes—very true—but you know that as soon as you came to this new scene, you thought I could be useful in giving you an insight into it, and in advising you. I have done so to the best of my power, have I not? so that you can be sure your fast friend."

"Indeed you are," said Elinor.

"Now you are not so sure of everybody—and unless you wish it very much ......"

"Oh! no; besides he can easily find the way if I tell him."

"Yes; and never mind saying much about it to anybody, that's my advice. It will be better just not to do it."

Elinor instantly agreed; and after this they talked on other subjects, about which, although Elinor laughed a great deal less than with Sir Peter, she was far more deeply interested, and forgot every one else, while his low voice, and her lower rejoinder was suffered to continue uninterrupted.

"Oh! that inveterate flirt!" said Sir Peter to Laura, by whose side he sat; and Laura with death in her heart, was cross to her cousin, and conveyed in obscure language, which had a clear meaning for him, that he did not help her, and was either clumsy or careless.

The boy was piqued at this, to strain his efforts for better success, and it was therefore with eagerness that he watched next morning, lest the promised walk should escape him; but, Leslie also had his attention alive, and in order to give Elinor a good excuse for not going out, he made use of a means, which no object less interesting could have induced him to bring into play. This was a literary effort of his own, a poem which he could willingly have read to a severe judge, who would have treated it according to its own faults or merits; but very unwillingly to an audience whose admiration was determined beforehand, by the fact that it was their guest and friend who wrote it.

Laura's eagerness to accept his offer was based on exactly this reason.

"D'ailleurs tous nos parens sont sages, vertueux."
BOILEAU.

"Oh! thanks, thanks, what a treat it will be! Peter, here's such a pleasure for you, Mr. Leslie is going to read a poem of his own to us. Oh! I am all impatience—such a treat."

"Nay," said Leslie, "how can you know that beforehand. I want your opinion whether the thing is good or not."

"Oh! there can be no doubt of that. Come to my morning room, where we shall not be interrupted; I could not endure any interruption. You don't mind Elinor, do you, she is there already."

"Not in the least," said the candid Leslie. Accordingly, to this select committee, he about half an hour after this time unfolded his MS., and told them it was a few verses, which he had a mind to send to a magazine then in fashion, to see whether they would be accepted or not.

"Of course they must," said Laura, "they will be only too happy to print anything you may write."

"If they don't," said Leslie, "I shall be mortified that my verses should be worse than those which they do print—but a man cannot judge for himself. I like them, but that is no test; I shall learn their value from your decision."

"I know THAT will be favourable," said Laura.

"And you, Miss Ladylift?" said Leslie, to Elinor.

"I can tell if I like them, or not; but that's all," said Elinor.

Leslie smiled, and Laura flattered herself he was comparing the childish simplicity of the young girl, with her own confidence in his genius. It was a poem of some ten or twelve quatrains, beginning, "I stood within the graves o'ershadow'd vault," verses which were afterwards sealed with public applause, and which delighted Leslie himself; but, he had no confidence that they would be approved by others. The approbation on this occasion was unbounded on the part of the mistress of the house; but the author was not at all touched by it, except so far as he considered it a homage to his own personal merits; indeed he thought none of them able to form any useful judgment, but he had a mind to hear what Elinor would say.

"It is too long, I think," said Elinor.

"Good heavens, too long!" cried Laura, "I only wish it were ten times longer."

Elinor coloured up to her eyes, at being thus convicted of misapprehension; but Leslie smiled brightly, and after a few seconds said she was quite right; as he read it, he had himself been struck by the necessity of cutting out some of the stanzas.

"It is very useful to read aloud what one has silently written," said he; "which do you think I must take away?"

Elinor answered nothing at all to this, and Leslie had not expected she could.

The morning had worn on meantime, and when the party seemed likely to disperse, Elinor had withdrawn to her room, and it was plain to Sir Peter that his chance was over for the present. He took Laura into the conservatory just outside, and here their conversation soon began to break into gleeful laughter, and exclamations of capital! and then hush! and foolish boy! Leslie paid no attention, but went his way, with his verses in his hand, remodelling what he thought faulty, and intent on showing the approving answer of the magazine when it should arrive, to his late audience.

In no long time after, he was summoned to luncheon, and then to an expedition which had been arranged to a neighbouring lion. When the ladies had gone upstairs to get their cloaks and bonnets, hats and habits, Laura followed Elinor into her room, and in a friendly tone asked whether she particularly wished to go to Gilbert's Glen.

"I should like it very much," said Elinor, not sure what answer the question meant to get.

"Oh! then of course it is settled—it does not signify."

"What does not? I am quite willing to stay at home."

"What, really!" said Laura; "are you certain?"

"Quite, if you prefer it."

"Nay, in that case, you could do me a service. I meant to have gone myself this morning, but Mr. Leslie's interesting poem prevented me. I want some specimens from the Neenshill quarry to show Mr. Goell to-night, and if you don't mind staying, you could get them while I am away."

"Is Sir Peter going to Neenshill?" said Elinor, speaking suddenly the thought that instantly occurred.

"Peter! no—he is to ride with me—what should take him there?"

Elinor coloured again, at her mistake, and willingly undertook Laura's commission. Pleased at her success, Laura descended the staircase, and found the party assembled in the hall, some for riding, some for driving.

"Isn't Miss Ladylift coming?" said Sir Peter.

"Well! do you know, she has changed her mind," said Laura; "she says she thinks the day too hot, though I don't know that it is hotter than it was. I can't persuade her, she thinks she had better stay quietly in her room—her head aches she says."

Thus glibly lying, Laura got into the phaeton, and the party set off.

Leslie had been appointed to drive Laura; therefore he saw nothing of the movements of the rest, till they arrived at the destined place, and assembled to walk up the glen; then both he and his companions missed Sir Peter.

"Oh! such a misfortune!" said one of the girls who had come on horseback, "that beautiful horse of Mr. Chanson's, which Sir Peter was riding, fell lame."

"Really," cried Laura, "how annoyed my brother will be."

"And Sir Peter thought best to ride it back gently, when we were about half-way."

"The best thing he could do," said Laura.

Leslie meantime spoke to the groom who had accompanied the riding party. "What's the matter with the horse?" said he, indifferently.

"Don't think there's nothing, sir," said the groom; "but Sir Peter took it quite on his-self."

Leslie feared Sir Peter had taken more interesting matter on his-self than conveying home a lame horse, and instantly he suspected Elinor of being a party to this pre-arranged lameness of Rampage; and he resolved to know what it all meant.

He followed the party who had walked forward into the glen, and expressing his admiration of the scene to Laura, said he should like to climb the right side of the valley, where the rocks were steepest, and would join her again at the farthest outlet; but, if he should not be arrived by the time they reached it, they were not to wait. Laura gave an easy assent, which was more than he expected; but he had been prepared to disregard any remonstrance she might make, and therefore at once struck away into the wood, and having lost sight of the rest, turned, and came straight to the inn where the horses were being put up. The present of a sovereign convinced the groom that it could do the horse he had ridden no harm to turn round and carry Mr. Leslie home, and that he, the groom, was to return in the vacated seat of the phaeton. Accordingly Leslie mounted and riding gently away for the first quarter of a mile gradually increased his horse's speed, till he was going at a good hand-gallop back on the road to Chanson Wood. Had Sir Peter been cautiously riding a lame horse, Leslie must have overtaken him, but he did no such thing, and this convinced him more and more that the sudden lameness was a mere fiction, fitting into the sudden headache which he believed to be equally fictitious.

When he came to the house, nobody was there—the servants knew nothing—had not seen Miss Ladylift go out or come in. Leslie had met with Rampage in the stableyard being led about quite cured of his lameness, but not yet of his perspiration; his own horse required similar cares, and the head groom uttered anathemas upon young gentlemen's "hignorance of orses," such as often follow upon young gentlemen's excited passions which the grooms leave out of the account when they attribute all to "hignorance."

Turning at once to the wood, Leslie strode along the path which led to the quarry, with all the feelings of an injured man, and in a very short time had reached the hill, the highest point of which contained the quarry. It was dotted with trees in natural clumps, growing from rocky ledges which broke out over the surface from top to bottom, and among these the path wound, appearing and disappearing in its descent to the level ground. He stood a moment at the bottom, feeling that his appearance in pursuit of his rival would not wear a very dignified aspect, and while this occurred to him, two figures emerged for a moment from the wood to an open space and again disappeared among the trees. Leslie's eyes were fixed on the next opening, devouring the space beforehand; again the figures came and vanished, but nearer and plainer, and near and plain enough to know they were Elinor and Sir Peter. Leslie ground his teeth—to be deceived was one of the bitter feelings-that a creature so guileless as she seemed should have deceived, and been believed by him, was another. He thought at first he would meet and confound her by mere silence—then he would have given much not to have returned, and not to be found out by her in such interest as to watch her.

Under this sudden thought he dashed into the thick of the wood, and there, from safe distances, again fixed his eyes on the path along which they must go. They passed very near, Sir Peter carrying her basket, and talking with great animation. Elinor's face was hidden by her great hat and veil; she was saying nothing as she passed, but how could she when her companion was so loquacious? enough, enough, she was walking with him! They passed on, and Leslie strode away, burying himself in the woods till nearly dinner time, and then dressed furiously, and came down to the drawing-room as placidly and calmly as if not one disturbed thought raged within.

"What became of you, Mr. Leslie?" said Laura; "did you lose your way in the glen?"

"No," said Leslie; "but I got so entirely away from the place where we were to have met, that I resolved to borrow your groom's horse, and ride home without waiting for you."

Laura let the subject drop. "Look here," she said, turning to the table; "Elinor has been so kind as to get me some fossils to show Mr. Goell this evening, and after all that tiresome man is not come. They are beautiful, are they not?"

"Very," said Leslie, and turned to Elinor. "You got as far as the stone quarry then," said he, in the blandest tone, "this hot day?"

Irreproachable as the voice was, it made her colour.

"Yes," she said, in a low voice; "but ......" the disjunctive conjunction was indicated, not spoken through, and Leslie, taking up two or three in his hand, said "You must have had a great weight to carry. Your arm must ache, does it not?"

"No," said Elinor; "for Si ......"

"I had the honour of sparing Miss Ladylift that trouble," said Sir Peter.

"Oh—yes!" said Leslie, as if the explanation were most satisfactory, and he would not catch the eyes of Elinor, which he felt sought his, to explain or deprecate, or deceive—he thought the latter.

And now for the next few days Leslie behaved like a brute to Elinor; a polished brute, bringing her shawl, setting her chair, opening the door with frigid politeness, but never once looking her in the face; never coming near for a word of explanation, never entering into what she said or did; never including her in any project or employment. All the time he felt he was straightening, rather than loosing the bond between them, for he was aware she was intent upon explanation, and that at any moment by a return to kindliness he could open all the pent-up feelings of that guileless heart; yes, guileless, for in his most secret thought he was convinced there was no guile in Elinor, though he chose to say, even to himself, there was.

Meantime, she was so unhappy that she sometimes rebelled against it; she seriously thought she would return to her convent, and hide herself from a world where plainly nobody cared for her. When all her efforts to speak to Leslie, and to conciliate him, failed—when he persevered in mortifying her, and in affecting unconsciousness of her presence, her heart rose quite full of tears, and seemed too swollen for her bosom.

"What right has he to make me so unhappy," she said to herself, but Leslie did not melt, though he saw her eyes cloud with what he knew were tears, suppressed though they might be.

Laura saw all this and was delighted; she thought her plans were working their full effect; and Leslie's attention to her, which was mostly aimed at vexing Elinor, she readily deceived herself into thinking was wholly to please herself. She was in great spirits; she looked very handsome, and did all that she could imagine would best please her favoured guest. His poem she continually brought forward till he dreaded the very mention of it. Every post, she remembered not to forget her interest about the expected answer, and each time she expressed her conviction that the editor would only not know how to give it sufficient welcome. Leslie felt confident enough of that also, but the pudeur of composition (when the author has written what he felt) made him shrink from so much talk about it. It was the fourth morning after his estrangement from Elinor that the letters as usual being brought round at breakfast, Laura's inquiry again broke in on Leslie's glance over those laid beside him. "Is there an answer yet?"—and he, breaking open the seal of a business-like looking one, ran his eye down the page, and replied in rather an unnecessarily indifferent tone,

"Yes, they refuse it." Laura had not much tact; instead of dropping so distasteful a subject, she could not let it alone.

"Impossible! how absurd! and the things they do take, yet refuse yours!—for my part I thought they would have seized upon it like a gold mine! Well they don't know their own interest."

"That is just what they do know," said Leslie; "what is likely to please, they are certain to adopt," and he folded each fold of the paper, and put it into his pocket.

"I only wish you would give it me," said Laura; "I would print it, and show the world what poetry is." So she went on, not conscious how this effort to show the author was not mortified, pressed on him the assurance that everybody saw he was.

Leslie, however, turned the matter into laughter, wished his enemy might write a book; and, in fact, took the rejection to heart very little after the first moment of making it public. But Elinor had seen that he was vexed for some instants, and when the ladies were lingering in the morning-room before separating for their several avocations, she had heard Laura making much of it to the circle round her.

"Poor Mr. Leslie," she said; "I'm sorry for Mr. Leslie, he bore it pretty well."

In the innocence of her heart, Elinor deduced that he had suffered a great fall, that he was humbled, he who had been so proud and lofty in every way. She glided away, unnoticed; and with a beating heart reached the door of the library, where Leslie was reading, forgetful, probably of the whole matter; or, if he thought of it at all, merely resolving to annihilate the editor some day or other, by giving all his support to the rival magazine. He did not look up, though he saw in a mirror opposite that it was Elinor, and his heart quickened its throb in consequence; but he would not relax from his unkindness.

She had laid her little plan for doing him a sort of homage, in what she looked upon to be adverse circumstances, and in pursuance of it had already sought for, and found a book, the only circumstance about which that interested her, was that the text in one page was mixed with a certain number of Latin verses, which verses she meant to be her allies in her harmless stratagem. Yet she hesitated for a minute before carrying her plan into execution, and in the mirror he contrived to watch her, without attracting her observation. He saw her timid approach, he marked the pause she made, and how she lightly pressed her small white teeth upon her under lip, like one in perplexity about the thing she was going to do. Presently she resolved to come forward, and did so hastily; upon which, Leslie rose, and was ceremoniously placing a chair for her, when she broke in.

"No, I don't want to sit down, I want to ask you if you will explain this Latin for me."

He took the book a little surprised at her request, and read into English four lines beginning— "Pannonis haud aliter post ictum sævior Ursa."

"Thank you," said Elinor, looking him in the face, "you know everything, you can do everything. How pleasant to be so clever as you are."

Leslie returned her look, trying to comprehend what this little scene meant.

"What book is it," said he, "where you have found this passage?" and he turned to the title page of the little volume. Elinor did not know; she held out her hand for it.

"It is," said she, "it is ......" and she tried to catch the title at the top of the page, Leslie saw in a moment that she knew nothing about it.

"Have you read it through, as far as this?" said he.

"Not quite," said Elinor.

"It is a volume of Montaigne's Essays," said Leslie. " What would the Reverend Mother say, if she knew you had such a book in your hands?"

"Would she be angry?" said Elinor, in sincerest alarm.

"Nay, does not it strike you as you read, especially now this twentieth Essay," (he knew perfectly well she had not read a word of it)—"that she would hardly have thought it a fit study for her pupil?"

"Would not she indeed," said Elinor, "Oh! indeed I did but just look at it a very little."

"If you had looked a very little more," said Leslie, "I should not have had the pleasure of being your interpreter, for here is the Latin done into French at the bottom of the page."

"Is there?" said Elinor, more embarrassed, "I did not think—that is I thought ......"

"You thought," said Leslie, his whole manner changing to tenderness, "that I was vexed, and you came to raise my self-esteem."

"No, no, not vexed," she murmured.

"Yes, indeed; do not deny it. I see it, like a glimpse of Paradise. How gentle, how womanly—all I could have aspired to, would have been forgiveness, for I have done very ill, but you no sooner fancy me humbled, than your generosity comes to put me higher than I was before."

"Indeed," said Elinor, "I wanted to know the meaning."

"Indeed no," said Leslie; "you had something better in view. You acted from the impulses of your noble heart. How inferior I am—despicable. If I might ever reach to your height—nay, do hear me, Elinor—I begin to know myself."

"I know you are good and clever," said Elinor.

"Good? alas! but I may become so. All good is possible in contact with such lovely goodness. Elinor! I cannot tell whether there is any feeling in your heart for me, beyond that which you would have for your father confessor; but in mine, there is a perfect love for you, which I did not know I was capable of. Love me! love me! Oh! Elinor, say you can love me enough to be my wife."

Elinor stood speechless, puzzled by his change of manner, uncertain whether he was displeased at first, amazed at his earnest expressions, and perfectly bewildered by the prayer to which it all led.

"How can I tell," she said, at last, and Leslie's earnestness earnestnesss increased with his uncertainty.

"Is there no answer for me but that," he said; "what does it mean, Elinor, am I such a stranger to all your thoughts, am I so indifferent to you, that you cannot tell whether you think kindly of me?".

"Oh yes! I can tell that," said Elinor, "you know you are my only friend."

"And is not your only friend fit to ask you for his only friend, the nearest, dearest friend—his wife?"

"That only Mr. Chanson can tell," said Elinor.

"Oh! your guardian? yes, I understand you now; but it is your answer, not his, that I want; Elinor, I am not asking your guardian to be my wife."

Elinor smiled, and her bright, shy eyes were kindled almost to laughter, but she answered with a grave voice. "It is only he, who can determine for me about such things."

"So they say in your convent," said Leslie, "but consider how many things were told you there, which differ from what you have learned in the world. Think, most precious Elinor, is it he who can tell, or you, whether you would be pleased at dwelling always where I dwell, at being as certain that my heart is full of you, as that you say your daily prayers, at making my life, (and yours with mine) good and happy; at knowing all I know, no secret ever between us, and if we have any trouble, having it together, and knowing exactly the measure and weight of each other's pain as well as pleasure?"

Elinor was silent, but she was listening to every word; her eyes had fallen from his, but her hand rested in the grasp of his two hands.

"Can any tell all this, except yourself? Can you not tell it now? answer me, only answer may I love you."

"I thought I had made you angry," said Elinor.

"Oh! never think that again—be my wife, and such thoughts could never come—there would be but one thought between us, neither you could doubt me, nor I you; would not there be a pleasure in that?"

"Yes," said Elinor, thinking, "he will never suspect me again," while through Leslie's mind it glanced—

"She played me false about that rendezvous with Bicester, but never mind, I won't tempt her to tell me stories." Aloud he said, "Then tell me your own self you are mine. Say there is so much happiness for me in this world, land for you too, happiness—is it not—will it not be?" and now his hand unforbidden got round her waist. Elinor began to understand him.

"Yes—it is more happiness than I ever thought of," she said; "but Mr. Chanson must say if I may."

"No, no; not yet, at least, you have nothing to ask from him; it will be enough that he should be told by and by. This is our own concern, that the world's. Why should they meddle, and whisper, and smile; to us it is serious, it is sacred? Why should every fool know our precious secret?"

Elinor was glad to be allowed silence, she would have felt it a painful task, to say anything so interesting to Mr. Chanson, to whom she never talked; or to Laura, of whom she was afraid; and she went out of that room full of a consciousness of the great thing that had happened, yet apparently as much the same quiet Elinor, as it was possible to be.

Leslie was equally self-controlled, he wished beyond measure to keep his secret, and therefore succeeded; there was no covert thought prompting either of them to let it be discovered, and therefore there was a perfect simplicity and good faith in their manner of doing it.

The days following were a time of incredible happiness to Leslie. He had been vanquished by generous and good feelings suddenly getting the mastery over him, and he was lifted above the base purposes which he had entertained towards Elinor. He enjoyed his own better feelings, the nobler part of his nature took the place of the baser, and had an artistic attraction for him; he felt himself freer for great things than before, he had the pleasure of loving what was not himself, yet his own; and although he was unable to conceive the guileless purity of the young girl, he was more and more captivated by the degree of it, which he could not help discerning, as he became more intimate with her thoughts and ways. Elinor was awakening to the hopes and happiness of life; the Being under whose influence these prospects unfolded themselves, became her one interest, and identified himself with all her feelings. She opened her heart to his love, and mused upon his home, his society, their position together as dwellers under one roof, mused with the innocence of a child which hears many things, but has no interpreter within, by which to understand them. She would have been contented with this state of things for an indefinite length of time, but Leslie began to entertain some remorse as to the part he was playing by Laura.

"She must be told," he said to himself. "It is due to her generous behaviour towards me, and my position as guest of her house. I will tell her, if nobody else."

Accordingly, one morning, when he knew her to be alone in her sitting-room, he bade Elinor make some pretence for going to her there, and when she had been in the room for a few minutes, he also knocked at the door, and on hearing permission, went in. Laura rose hastily, with a look of sudden wonder, and of some other emotion which prompted her to get rid of Elinor by all means.

"Have you found what you want, dear child," she said; "there, yes, that's it, is not it? ......" but Leslie interrupted her.

"Nay," he said, "it was I who told—begged, that is, her to be here. We want your concurrence." He observed, though without fixing his eyes on Laura's face that there was a kind of horror in it, such as comes when an object of phantom-like dread rises before one, and the mind refuses to believe it. He immediately finished his sentence. "This lady," Leslie indicated Elinor, "consents to be my wife. I owe it to you that you should be the first informed."

The blood forsook Laura's lips; her heart it was plain had stopped, so far as a heart can stop which is to go again. The nerves relaxed, so that the strong will could hardly make instruments of them; but she did force them to act. She smiled as some one among us may have seen a dying man attempt to smile when the power over his muscles was half departed; she looked on both with eyes where were no tears, the conventionalities of society held them back. Leslie went on speaking, without appearing to observe her.

"And now we shall look to your kind offices for counsel and assistance in our project, and for making known to the world in general what we thought it right to bring first to the best friend of both."

"Not yet," said Laura, speaking with a steadily, uniform voice; "my brother has so little thought of such a thing, that he would, perhaps, throw obstacles in the way."

"Obstacles!" said Leslie, carelessly.

"No, not that, but he might be angry with her I mean; it would so disturb him."

"Believe me," said Leslie; "we are both willing to leave it to you to make the discovery when you like. Neither of us shall interfere on that subject, if one way or another seems better to you."

"It is merely your advantage I think of," said Laura.

"Of that I am QUITE sure," said Leslie: in order to convey some pleasant impression to Laura's mind.

"And now," he said, "I'll leave my little betrothed with you to get some woman's talk about fringe and so on. She wants a friend on all matters as you well know, and I humbly beg for one than whom she could not anywhere find a better." Leslie drew back, courteously applying his compliment by a slight indication of his head, and quitted the room, after an encouraging glance at Elinor.

When he was gone, the agitation of the scene acted upon Elinor, and she could not restrain her tears, while she tried to possess herself of Laura's hand, but Laura's efforts were exhausted; she drew away her hand as if it had come in contact with a fester, or a nest of snakes, and forcing open the door to her bed-room flung it behind her, and fell on the floor by her bed, totally giddy and beside herself for a brief time. In some people, their first thought under a sudden shock is, that the thing is not; or that it will cease to be. In the worst of her anguish this latter idea spread a gloomy light through the thick darkness, otherwise no strength of hers could have supported it. It was that which by degrees gave consistency to her thoughts, and upon which her mind as tenaciously laid hold, as the falling man, on the bush which grows over the edge of the precipice. She collected her senses and forced her mind into action, not with any view ever entertained for a moment of making the best for herself and others of what had taken place, but with the desperate purpose of destroying it at no matter what sacrifice.

The first thing was to gain time, and this her instinct had already prompted her to do, when she besought Leslie to keep the secret for awhile. What was to follow she ran over in her head, and sate in her tranquil room, among all, the pretty luxuries of toilette and draperied mirror, of flaçons and flowers, leaning her rounded cheek on her hand, while the natural folds of rich silk fell around her figure, and all this time was brooding the project which should immolate the innocent girl, and the beloved man to the idol enshrined in her own person.

To this end she laid her plan, and with farsighted anticipation she soon after sought her brother, and engaged him by gentle degrees in a conversation on his political interest, which had always a certain charm for him. There was some property at a little distance lately acquired by him, where the votes of the tenants were less their landlord's than those which had longer felt his subject of discourse, and suggested the propriety of "at some future time, any leisure day," cultivating their acquaintance and gaining a hold on their opinions.

Her brother assented, but complained of the tediousness of the operation. Laura hinted that he should lighten the disgust by taking a companion; some one, she said, who would do credit to the cause, and whom he might recommend to them whenever there was occasion.

"Why not speak out," said Mr. Chanson; "there is one I should be glad enough to recommend, if you can tell me you wish it."

"Nay, you know all I know about him," said Laura.

"All?"

"Yes, and far more than any other human being ever can know."

"Then I wish it were more, for my dear little Laura is not the woman to be trifled with."

"No, no, don't say such a word. I understand him, and so he does me. Only be best friends with him, and give him an interest among us."

"I will do anything for you, sister," said he; "you are as clever as you are handsome, and deserve the very best man wit and money can gain. I shall be sorry to part with you, that is all. But if you gain by it, I won't think of myself."

"Thank you, Lawrence," said Miss Chanson, and the kindness breathed over her heart like dew upon some burning, arid plain. The tears came to her eyes, and she hid them on his shoulder.

"You are happy, Laura?" said he, inquiringly; "you are satisfied?"

"Yes," said Laura; "oh, yes, I am." It was very hard to form those words, but she succeeded.

She had provided in this manœuvre for securing the absence of Leslie whenever her plans should require such a movement to work out the present details. She had only her cousin Peter to help her, and in the late circumstances of apparent estrangement between Leslie and Elinor, he had been laid aside as not wanted. Now, however, he was her chief hope; and the day of his departure drawing very near, what he had to do must be done without delay.

"Peter," she said, "we are all going to walk after luncheon. Now that little flirt will enjoy a tête-à-tête with you. I really think she begins to get an appetite for it."

"Do you think so," said her cousin; "well she shows it in an odd way. How uncommonly silent she is, except to Leslie."

"Oh! she torments him to death," said Laura, "he was saying to me this morning that he wished— wished—that is ......"

"What, Laura?"

"He came, Peter, to my room to speak to me; and she was there, and would not go away."

"My dear Laura!"

"No, no, nonsense; I don't know what he had to say, but with her in the room, and so determined to stay ......"

"Yes, yes; but during the walk this afternoon there may be a better opportunity. Well, cousin Laura, you know it will break my heart, but I devote myself, I cover my head with a white mantle, and stretch out my hands to the infernal gods."

"What nonsense you talk, dear Peter."

"Shall we take a gentle walk in the woods?" said Laura, to the party after luncheon, "the autumn colours are growing beautiful, and the day is neither too hot nor cold."

Everybody agreed, and they assembled gradually under the portico, as they were ready, previous to the start. Leslie had gently driven Laura into a corner, and in the fulness of contentment with himself and others, was asking questions sufficiently embarrassing.

"Have you taught her, Miss Chanson, how to cut out cloaks and gowns; and what to do with a housekeeper?"

Laura commanded her voice, and made some trifling answer.

"You know it is to you only I can talk on the subject," Leslie went on; "in the first place, I have no mind to let everybody into my affairs, and in the next, you bid me be silent for the present."

"Oh yes! be silent," said Laura, "I have more reasons than one for that request. Pray say nothing yet."

"That you command me is sufficient reason," said Leslie, who felt that he owed her some reparation.

"You yourself, perhaps, may find reason to thank me," said Laura.

"Nay, I thank you already. The one point being gained, of security in the regard of that little lady, I am grateful for every evidence of interest in either her, or me."

"How happy you are in a confiding, honest nature," said Laura.

"People always despise those whom they call confiding" said Leslie, "and those despised persons always presume on their own particular clear-sightedness, and say others may be taken in, but as for them it is impossible."

"Heaven forbid, that it should happen to you!" said Laura, then hastily went on. "You talk so loftily about despising, and being despised, like one who knows there is no such word for him; but come, the party is all assembled now I think."

She moved a step forward, and so did Leslie, and saw that Elinor was standing just within the door, and that the officious Sir Peter had offered her his arm for the walk. Laura eagerly watching also, perceived that Elinor lifted her eyes to Leslie, and that a slight glance of intelligence passed between them, after which Elinor demurely took the offered arm, and proceeded with Sir Peter. That look wrenched the dagger round in Laura's heart; it was the thing which her imagination had represented as most intolerable, the familiar token which both understood, and from which all others were shut out; her insidious words had fallen useless, and now, friendly as Leslie might be, faithfully as he kept by her side, he did but confirm her anguish by a behaviour which was so friendly, merely because he had made her the confidant of his successful love for another. She could not play out her part to the end to-day. She was obliged to complain of a headache before the walk was over, and sank into silence, which this excuse justified, and which with her throbbing head and dry lips, it was impossible for her to avoid. When they reached home again, she went straight to her room, and appeared no more, accepting Elinor's timid offers of service, in order to keep her away from the society of Leslie.

For a time she preserved the impenetrable silence which her feelings dictated and which Elinor, frightened at the repulses she met, shrank into herself to observe; but at last, as she slowly won self-command, she resolved to employ the time in preparing the ground for the scheme before her, and however odious to herself to enter into conversation with the happy young girl.

"How was this all arranged, dear?" she began, in an invalid tone, "tell me about it."

Elinor was as little inclined as she to pour out confidences, but she hesitated not to answer.

"I was afraid he was angry," she began ......

"Well," said Laura, impatiently.

"I was afraid he was unhappy," said Elinor.

"What do you mean?" again said Laura, hastily.

"He seemed angry."

"Oh! nonsense—what stuff—what made him angry?"

"Your cousin ......" Elinor began, but was glad to be interrupted by her imperious sympathizer.

"By the by, I wanted to speak about Peter; he is a very young man, and you must not make mischief. You have been talking a great deal with him, you know that surely; and flirting, the world would say, and now that another man is going to marry you, that man may take fancies against Peter; you must say nothing against Peter, that's the only reparation you can make."

"I have never ......"

"Yes, you have—never mind that. Have you talked to Mr. Leslie about that time when you stayed at home on account of a bad headache you had, and then walked to the stone quarry?"

"Had I a bad headache?"

"Yes, of course, you can't forget that."

"I don't think ......"

"Yes, very bad, you did not drive with me to the glen on account of it."

Elinor was silent.

"Have you talked to him about it? I say."

"No."

"Oh! that's very well, then do not. I know that you and Peter went together."

"No ...... he ......"

"Well, came back together, from the stone quarry, and if you were to make a long story about it to Mr. Leslie, there is no knowing what might happen. It was foolish, perhaps thoughtless that is, in my dear cousin, but merely that, scarcely that; and Mr. Leslie is so proud, he might take the greatest offence, he might shoot him dead, my poor cousin."

"Might he really?" said Elinor.

"So promise me one thing, never to say one word about that walk—now promise."

"I never will, if I can help it."

"Oh! you can help it of course. Promise."

"I promise, as far as I can," said Elinor.

"Can! ridiculous! however, that will do, and now pray let me be quiet. I really cannot talk any more, my poor head in such a state."

And now putting her hand to her head, she leaned it down against the back of her easy chair, and there in anything but ease, she acted the motionless invalid, in which character she could escape further conversation, yet retain the young girl as nurse, and watch in her room. This lasted till bed time, and a severe trial it was.

When at last she had dismissed Elinor, with severe directions to go at once to her chamber, and had got rid of the importunate services of her maid, she was at liberty to start up, and walking through her room, to give vent to the bodily expressions of the tempest in her mind. The one fixed purpose was that the marriage of Elinor and Leslie should be prevented. She had ceased to justify that purpose to herself, and had reached the point when the right or wrong was cast aside, and the end only, kept resolutely in view. When all the house was quiet, when her brother had come, and tenderly stroked her hair, asking how his little Laura did now; when he was gone, carefully closing the door without noise behind him, Laura unlocked her desk, pressed the spring of the secret drawer within, and took out a slip of written paper, poor Elinor's note to Leslie, which had fallen on the ground the night of their interview in the wood. And there in the early hours, between night and morning, when she ought to have been stretched in maiden slumber on her bed, when she ought to have been profiting by the safety and the indulgence of her prosperous position, Laura sat cold and weary, yet absorbed from such feelings, patiently effacing by the smallest advances one letter after another from the harmless billet, in order to replace them by others which should carry condemnation to the guiltless writer. Her brother's name was the word she rubbed out; and then with a pen, prepared with the most delicate touches of the knife, and tried twenty times before it suited her, Leslie's was the one she put in. Now it stood—

"I cannot come to-night. Mr. Leslie forbids me to go out.—ELINOR LADYLIFT."

This note thus altered, she purposed to convey to Sir Peter as coming from Elinor, and from him it should pass either by Sir Peter, or by Laura herself to Leslie, whom she trusted it would persuade of Elinor's falsity, and by so doing wrench two hearts asunder. There were chances of an explanation between them, and that Laura saw with fearful distinctness; should it take place, her plot was ruined, and she herself with it—where should she be then?

"Hated, despised!" she cried to herself; "for ever parted from him. But so I am now. Can it be worse than to see her in my place. Oh! nothing is worse. Death were most dear in comparison ......" and as she said so, tears of self-compassion broke from her eyes, and she laid her head on her arms and wept. Presently she rose from this position, and letting her dressing-gown fall from her shoulders, put one knee on her luxurious bed, and laid herself down beneath the fine woollen, fine linen of the bed clothes.

"Alas!" she said to herself, "if the felicity which I labour through all obstacles to attain were mine by the gracious course of fortune and fate, how good I could be, how kind to others, how grateful myself!"

CHAPTER VIII

The next morning, after breakfast, Leslie contrived to say to Elinor, that he had been unjustly deprived of her society the previous evening, and that she must come out and walk with him.

"Miss Chanson can say nothing against it," he added; "for you need only answer her that you are going with your affianced husband, and her brother won't think of us one way or the other."

"Besides," said Elinor, "he will be at the stable for the next half hour, and Miss Chanson will have the housekeeper almost directly. I can come down the turret stair and out by the great Datura."

"We are doing all we can to spoil the most guileless nature in the world," said Leslie to himself; "when she came here, such a woman's calculation as that was out of the reach of her imagination. Well, well, she is a creature of whom I am most unworthy, be she spoiled a little or not."

In about a quarter of an hour Elinor did as she had proposed and joined him in the garden, and then seizing her hand he led her into the park and out thence to the fields, and soon they were quite away from all frequented track. It was an autumn day, the heavy mists were golden with the sun which was vigorously dispelling them from the valleys and brook courses, and lifting them up all gorgeously from the glowing earth. The red berries of the wild convolvulus hung in long festoons upon the hedges, and its yellow leaves shone like pale gold in the sun. The wild cherry trees were glowing with bright red, the birch all amber; the ferns dressed the hill sides with their rich shapes and colours, and the hills drew nearer than usual, with every white house and spire distinct on their intense blue. A fragrance of vegetation came and went on the breeze; perhaps it was the breath of dying Nature, but it pleased the lungs with its exciting draught.

"I feel my heart beating" said Elinor; "at seeing everything so beautiful. Why does it beat?"

"Because everything is so beautiful," said Leslie, smiling.

"And you told me I might enjoy the pleasure," said Elinor.

"Yes, it is fitted to give enjoyment. It is innocent; you feel no regret afterwards."

"No, I don't," said Elinor; "but I should have done so in my convent, because I was taught to fear the things I liked. It was you who taught me differently."

"Yes; but at all events do whatever you think is right," said Leslie. "I only meant to say that whatever is good and pleasant you may do."

"I think" said Elinor, "that walking through this autumn country, and my hand held by yours is both."

"Both, both," said Leslie; "and it will soon be our right for ever. We shall be never parted, Elinor; never, not at all, together always, and it will be right to be so; do you understand?"

"Yes," said Elinor, her calm, maidenly face looking straight forward; "there will be no stranger to interrupt our talk, no necessity to ask anybody's leave to walk with you. I may sit in the room where you write, and work without talking; when you like, I may sing what you only like; if you are tired you can sleep without caring whether I am there or not, and I shall be there watching that neither the sun nor the flies disturb you. I have been thinking of all those things."

Leslie was silent. It was a new, strange pleasure to hear the meditations of that innocent heart. He believed at that hour what so very few men have the enjoyment of believing, the purity and guilelessness there can be, and is, in many young girls. His pleasure was like that of a man who gets sight of an unsunned treasure, which the earthly air and light he lets in will soon crumble away; but which is there and has been there in perfection, for all the time before he discovered it. The loveliness of the day, the accidents of the scene gave scope to the easy happiness they were enjoying. It grew hot, and Elinor untied her bonnet in the shade, and Leslie took it from her to carry, maltreating the ribbons as he talked and walked, and then laughing with Elinor at his male ignorance of their nature and wants. They came to a steep slope, and beginning to move quicker and quicker down it, ended by running at the top of Elinor's speed, so that laughing, and the blood mounting in her cool cheek, she came to the bottom holding tight by Leslie's arm, while he kept her safely on her feet, and laughed with her at nothing but their own spirits, and their own active frames.

There, as they coasted along a high bank with an irregular hedge on the crest, Elinor's eye was caught by something hounding about in the fern, and in a moment they saw it was a leveret which seemed at play so near them. Elinor paused to look, but Leslie saw how it was, and said it was caught in a noose, and the string was tightening round its neck.

"Oh! how cruel, how wicked!" said Elinor; "who could! loose it do, pray." Leslie, to obey Elinor, went up the bank and tried to lay hold of the leveret, which, half dead as it was, still sprang about to avoid him.

"It will die," cried Elinor, the tears almost running over; "oh! do catch it," and she also scrambled up, and helped Leslie to try to lay hold of it. At last they succeeded. Then Leslie, with one hand upon the suffocated little beast, searched his waistcoat pocket for a knife, and gave it to Elinor to open, and to insinuate it between the leveret's neck and the string in order to set it free. He watched her earnest face, all given over to pity and interest; her fear to give pain, her resolution to venture it, her disgust at suffering inflicted; and she, thinking of nothing but the leveret, most delicately, most skilfully got in the knife, and drawing the sharp edge across the string released it. The poor leveret, under the sudden revulsion of blood to its natural course, lost all active power, and lay motionless.

"Poor brute, it's all over," said Leslie, putting it on the grass; but Elinor was not so indifferent. She raised its head upon a little tussock, stroked it gently, pitied it, while her lover stood by smiling at the pretty picture; and at last the leveret began to move, and Elinor was relieved and delighted.

"Oh! I'll carry it home," she said, breaking off a great burdock leaf, and placing the little body upon it; then carefully set it on her arms, and Leslie held her by the elbow, to get her safely down the bank. "I'll get what they call a whisket for it," said Elinor, pleased like a fresh child with the imaginary details of the leveret's life; "and keep it in my room, and give it leaves. What does it like best?"

"Flowers, I think," said Leslie; "any fresh, tender annuals out of the garden. It will eat up the verbenas with the greatest pleasure."

"Do you think you can get some?" said Elinor.

"Oh yes, every morning; but I must take care Miss Chanson does not see me."

"Oh! you must not hurt her garden."

"Well, well; we will take the hare away with us, when you and I go away ourselves, and it shall have all the flowers at the Tower to itself, if you like."

Elinor looked at Leslie, and smiled. "Yes, thank you; it shall live on the eastern terrace you told me of, and have a wooden house of some kind to go into at night."

"That will be the very place," said Leslie.

At this moment the leveret, which had recovered its senses, but kept the recovery to itself watching its opportunity, made so sudden a spring, that before Elinor could utter the little cry its movement provoked, it was out of her arms, and scudding away to the copse.

"Oh dear!" said Elinor, looking at her empty leaf.

Leslie laughed.

"Never mind, I can have your hand again; so all is for the best," said he.

And thus they walked, by the hedgerow sides of the corn fields, across banky meadows cropped by sheep, along woodland paths, which descended to the brook courses; where they were crossed by gray large stepping-stones; within the edges of the wood, where with trees for a natural colonnade, they looked out upon the silent, sunny country; hand in hand they walked, healthy, beautiful, good. It was Adam and Eve moving through the Garden of Eden.

They had scarcely met a human being, the country was thinly inhabited, and they had unconsciously sought the least frequented parts; but some hours after they first began their walk, the forest silence was disturbed by a distant voice, uttering a loud "mark!" and then was fired a gun as distant, and before long both sounds came nearer; nay, they presently saw a towering pheasant hit by the discharge from the loud gun, and tumbling over and over in the air, fall with hanging wings, and dropped head, out of sight in the underwood.

The next moment, Sir Peter Bicester, and a gamekeeper, and couple of beaters came in view; he immediately left off his pursuit, and came up to Elinor, hoping he had not frightened her, and so on. Leslie had dropped Elinor's hand; till she was declared his promised wife, he did not wish to claim any intimacy with her; but Elinor was unconscious of such scruples, and replied in the simplest way to the young man's apologies.

"But we are going home now," she said, "so do not stop your amusement for me. Thank you for thinking of it." And she moved on.

"Shan't you come out, Leslie?" said Sir Peter.

"No, not I; if there's anything better to do, I don't care for a gun."

"And there is something it seems," said Sir Peter.

"Well! that is as it may be," answered Leslie, and followed Elinor, whom he speedily overtook.

CHAPTER IX

That evening, Sir Peter knocked at the door of his cousin's sitting-room, when he came in an hour before dinner.

"Have you got some tea, Laura?" he asked; "let me have a cup with you, if you are going to have any."

"Come in, come in!" said Laura, ringing the bell at the same time, and ordering tea for him and her. " Well, what have you shot?"

"Six pheasants, and a woodcock," said Sir Peter; "I just went into that outside cover, you know, below the lime kiln."

"And quite enough," said Laura, "for a distant part, scarcely preserved."

"Yes, it is a good way off," said Sir Peter; "and do you know, Leslie had taken your ward walking all that way."

"He had?"

"Yes, and they looked as like real lovers as ever you saw any two people. Now, Laura, I want you to answer me one question; are you quite certain there is nothing between them, quite certain? Because if there is, I would not put myself in their way for the generalship of the Indian army—no, not to be made knight banneret on the field of battle."

"Have not I told you," said Laura, "how matters stand."

"Yes; but he may be a fool, and he may have taken up with the little idiot; and if the flirting is not on her side, I will have nothing to do with making her break her little heart."

"It is all, all on her side; but for her intrigues I should be happy—and I can be happy—I am; what is that man to me?"

"Nothing, Laura; that's right, don't throw away a thought upon him, if he has been such an ass."

"But he has not!" said Laura, struggling mentally against the doom, as one does bodily against the great weight that is pressing the lungs together, so as to stop breath. "It is merely that a child is artful enough to deceive him, is thoughtless enough to hazard her own character, and ruins my peace."

"Nay, if it is so ......"

"I tell you it is."

"Swear!" said Sir Peter, crossing the forefingers of his two hands, playfully, yet in his heart looking seriously to such an appeal as safe to procure him the truth. Laura did not think nor hesitate for a moment. She laid her hand on his crossed fingers—

"I swear!" she said. She hated her cousin for making her do this, but she had no doubt, nevertheless, about doing it.

"Very well, then, I will serve you loyally and zealously to the extent of my power, and that extent is limited, for I must go on Thursday."

"Yes, yes, go on Thursday," said Laura, "and before that time, let Leslie merely see whether or not her pretended passion for him is true, only let her show herself in her true colours, that is all I ask."

"As how?"

"Well, if she appoints you to meet her? If she tampers with you, as she does with Leslie?"

"Oh! in that case."

"You will let him know it?"

"No, I shall not tell him—that's quite impossible."

"He can find it out then," said Laura.

"It would be better for him if he did; would lose a trifle and gain a treasure. Oh! Laura, I wish I were but older, wiser, or of more value in the world, I would fling myself at your feet, though Crœsus and Lycurgus were in the way."

"And I would not have you," said Laura, peevishly, then correcting herself, she added, "what a hoary pair to offer to a young lady; you would have a much better chance my Pet."

Sir Peter went on talking nonsense, which he much preferred to plotting against Elinor, for of that employment he was getting rather tired, and Laura was afraid to weary him entirely of the subject, for upon his co-operation all her remaining hopes depended. She therefore treated the subject as lightly as she could, only insisting on some display of despair on his part at his approaching separation from Elinor, and contriving to amuse him with details, each of which she hoped would be a blow against the security in which she saw that Leslie was fortified.

She herself conducted the assault this evening. Leslie gave her occasion; he told her that he must very soon announce to her brother the engagement into which his ward had entered; and Laura, now thoroughly on her guard assented, proposing that the end of the week should be the time chosen. Leslie agreed, and Laura had gained one point, for did not the Thursday of Sir Peter's departure come between?

"I shall be glad when he is gone for your sake," said Laura to Leslie.

"Why so?"

"Nay, I think you deserve all the walks and talks and little appointments to yourself."

"Oh, I am not uneasy about that," said Leslie; "such fancies trouble me not. As King Pericles says, 'Falseness cannot dwell in thee!'"

"Falseness in me?" said Laura, startled.

"In her, I ought to have said, but I was too conscientious to misquote Shakespeare. Oh! no, that trouble is quite over."

"Then why did she and my cousin find themselves at the stone quarry that day she had the sudden headache, and could not drive with us?"

"I'm sure I don't know," said Leslie; "the best way would be to ask her."

"Do, if you think the truth so easy to be had."

"Only I don't care to know," said Leslie.

"Oh! very well. I am sure I don't," said Laura.

She turned away, and proposed music to one of the party, but her eyes did not fail to observe that Leslie took advantage of the opportunity to stand talking with Elinor at the open window, and she persuaded herself was asking the explanation she intended him to seek. There was some little pre-occupation in his way of carrying on the beginning of the conversation, a shade of embarrassment, and a questioning air. Elinor coloured deeply, and hesitated to answer him, and Laura believed that the headache which she herself had ordered Elinor to remember, and the silence which she herself had ordered Elinor to keep about the stone quarry walk, were throwing the appearance of double-dealing over the entangled girl. Leslie's fond look at last she could not so well interpret. She did not think he was satisfied with respect to the walk, yet "perhaps" (thought she), "he believes a woman cannot speak the truth, and forgives her—forgives her; yes, but he would not forgive me."

Laura was not much out in her interpretation of Leslie's looks; in fact, he was disposed to believe and to excuse in Elinor, the manœuvres which he fancied the inexperienced young girl had been led to practise before her present engagement with him; but at all events, as things were now, he determined to put a stop to all proceedings of the kind, and would fain have warned and set Elinor on her guard, as her mother would have done, had she ever known her mother.

"Nobody may interrupt me now," he said, "in the happiness of such walks as we had yesterday. Nobody has any claim on you now, when I claim you. You have given me that right, remember."

"Mr. Chanson said I must go with him to see his greyhounds fed," said Elinor; "but I will not."

"Oh! Mr. Chanson. Yes, you may go with him."

"Miss Chanson also said I was to carry the hymn books to the school. She wants to show me how to teach them to sing. I will tell her I cannot do it."

"No, no; you must do what she asks till you leave her altogether."

"But you said I was to walk with you only."

"I mean it is not fit for a young girl to let an idle young man like Bicester, meet and follow her."

"So my Reverend Mother told me, and I did not, till you laughed, and made me laugh too, about it."

"Well, well, yes; but a man says things he does not mean; you should be aware that he does not even remember many things he says, and if a girl does, and believes it is all true, she gets into a very awkward position."

"You are a young man," said Elinor, smiling; "am I to believe you?"

"Oh! it is quite a different thing with me. What I say now, does not apply to me. Only I don't want you. to let that puppy talk to you. He can, only mean mischief, and you had better be on your guard."

"So the Reverend Mother said," repeated Elinor; "and I will obey her and you."

"Next Thursday he goes away," said Leslie; "and do you know, dearest and gentlest Elinor, that I am going too? Chanson has got a project in his head about visiting some property he bought not long ago; and he says his sister thinks it will be a good opportunity to do so when young Bicester leaves the house, and before fresh guests come in. He wants me so very much to be his companion, that I have consented. We shall not be away above a few days, and during those days I will tell him that his ward is his ward no longer, but that it is I who have to answer for her in future."

"Do," said Elinor.

Leslie looked at her, and half laughed. "You will not tell him the contrary?" said he.

"Oh! no, no," said Elinor; "no more, surely, will he? I am sorry though that I did not ask him first if I might, for the Reverend Mother told me it was my guardian who must settle that."

"And I told you not; very true. But you do not think I told you to do anything wrong?"

"I hope not," said Elinor, "for I have no right or wrong in my head now, except what I learn from you."

"Ay! trust me, then ...... Oh! I could not mislead you."

"No, I am sure of that," said Elinor, lifting her eyes to his. He thought of the morning at breakfast, when he could not get one glimpse of those shy eyes; and he thought also of the many things between that moment and the one in which her innocence had converted all his thoughts into pure projects like itself. In his heart he worshipped the creature who held so strong, yet so silken a dominion over him, and in his enjoyment of the prospect now before him, he instinctively tried to forget the cruel one which he had entertained and abandoned.

Laura had no time to spare, or she would have let things work more gently than she could now afford. This was Saturday evening; and the evening of Sunday she destined to commence a plot which must explode before Thursday, or all her schemes would be at fault. The course of Sunday contented her well enough. The usual duties of the day went forward, and however mechanically to Laura, there was no outward dereliction. She would have had a vague uneasiness at absenting herself from the village church, but no word that she heard there struck her as forbidding—no word she uttered there, struck her as renouncing—the secret purposes she meditated. Once, as a very young child, instructed to lay by every secular employment on the Sabbath day, it chanted that her mother, who led a usually secluded life, was invited by a very great house to very great feast on a Sunday; and the mother went, not because she thought and explained that there was no harm in it, but because the temptation was so strong. Laura had opportunities enough to melt down the impression which this fact made on her; nor did it, probably, in itself produce much effect, but her nature had that bias which caused it to select and feed upon this and various similar incidents which the tide of things presented to her, until at length led away by selfishness and by uncontrolled passions, she had come to be, as one may say, two Lauras, the one who professed in theory whatever was good, and the one whose actions regarded simply what was convenient. It is a very common character.

This Sunday, therefore, saw her in the family pew with her guests; saw her take the school report from the hand of the curtseying schoolmistress, and rebuke the child who was shown up for inattention. She let the horses and servants rest to-day, and proposed merely a walk by way of amusement. Before she could prevent him, Leslie drew Elinor away, and by the side of the waterfall and up the banks of the brook, they passed the afternoon hours.

Laura had got a present for her cousin Peter, a travelling bag, fitted in the smallest compass with the most numerous articles, and called him to her sitting-room to give it.

Sir Peter was rather melancholy and sentimental. He was going to the other side of the world, and was pleased to do so, and yet it touched him to feel that nobody was much interested in his departure except himself; his place would close over at once, and it was he only who cared or reflected that he was going. Laura's care, therefore, to procure a present for him, gave him pleasure. He employed himself in examining and admiring every article, and in obtaining from Laura a few words in her own hand, declaring herself the giver of the bag, and the well-wishing cousin of the recipient.

"And you will think of me once or twice, will you?" said Sir Peter; "when my thoughts are travelling homewards they will now and then meet yours coming out to Ceylon."

"To be sure they will; and many others will be on the same journey, anxious to know what you are about."

"No, Laura, no. My mother, if she were alive, would have let no post go by without a letter. I have a green bag stuffed with those she wrote to me at school, and so would a sister, perhaps, if I ever had one, but nobody else ever cares for a young man more than for one grain of wheat rather than another in a sack full."

"Oh! indeed, I do," said Laura, "and I am not the only one."

"Who else?"

"Nay, I don't think I shall tell you. It is such nonsense."

"You don't mean the little nun?"

"No, no; of course not."

"You do," said Sir Peter, starting up, and forgetting his melancholy; "what did she say?"

"Oh! nothing—I forget—nothing worth hearing."

"Nay, Laura, you shall tell me, or I will ask her. Where is she?"

"In her own room, I should think. You can't go there and ask her."

"I thought she was walking with Leslie."

"Not very likely after what she said to me. If she is walking with Mr. Leslie her coquetry passes all allowable bounds."

"Why, what did she say?"

"Nay, you will be so vain."

"Not vainer than I am," said Sir Peter, smiling gaily.

"True; that's hardly possible," said Laura; "well, well, she is very demure, and does not talk much you know, to me at least, but she said this morning in her sudden way, as if her words broke out of her thoughts, 'Sir. Peter smokes every evening, does not he?'"

"What an unsentimental meditation!" said Sir Peter.

"I did not think so," said Laura.

"As how, is it not?"

"When you smoke, you walk out; when you walk out you can be met."

"Nay, is that it? nice little girl!"

"I don't know that it is that, but it would be easy to make the experiment. If it is so, and she likes you Peter, do take her with you to Ceylon. I use no concealment. I should be glad if she were gone."

"Thanks, thanks, dear cousin, but I can't be quite so convenient as that, for I suppose you would have her my wife."

"Peter!"

"But if she do think of morning walks with Leslie, and moonlight walks with me, at least he will never marry her."

"Never, never, never!" said Laura.

Dinner was not over till the evening was dark, for October was at the end of its first week. The rooms were bright with lamps and candles, but the windows were open to the shadowy scene without, for the weather was very hot, even as though summer were abroad masquerading in the splendidly coloured robes of the aged year.

"Let us walk down the garden," said Laura to Elinor, who was the only lady beside herself of the party; "the air is oppressive, further from the house it will be cooler."

They went together along the garden paths, and reached the avenue of great Scotch firs which terminated it, and which at its other extremity had a wicket opening into the park.

"I wonder," said Laura, "whether Eliza Mosterick has had the broth she wanted; did you hear anything about it?"

"No, I did not."

"But you knew she was ill. Did you call to inquire about her when you were out this morning?"

"No," said Elinor.

"You might just as well have done so, and put the Sunday to some better purpose than merely amusing yourself," said Laura; "poor woman, perhaps she has been waiting vainly all day. I wish I could go as far before my brother comes into the drawing-room; he does not like me to be absent."

Elinor was silent; whatever she might say she felt would bring down a rebuke.

"Could you go, Elinor?" said Laura, at last.

"Certainly," said Elinor, who was accustomed at the convent to wait on the sick, and to be employed about their errands. "Shall I?"

"Well, if you will. You know the house; it is the underkeeper's—you know, just fifty yards from the end of the avenue on the right—she was very ill—unless she is better—and I meant to send her some broth and things .... Stay, take her five shillings will you, in case she wants to buy anything. Here, put my scarf over your head. It is as good as a bonnet."

Elinor did all she was bid, and Laura, when she was disappearing like a white spirit down the gloomy avenue, turned hastily and ran to the house, where she gave thanks (like Shylock when his enemies' ships are lost, and he says, "Thank God, I thank God!") to see that the time for evening Sunday prayers was not more than a quarter of an hour distant, at which epoch of the evening the absence of any member of the party must become conspicuous. Both Leslie and Sir Peter glanced round the room as soon as they came in, for Elinor. Both looked at Laura to account for her absence. A faint smile, and a slight elevation of her eyebrows informed the latter that Elinor would be found where he expected, and

Sir Peter vanished to keep the imaginary rendezvous on his side. Leslie asked in a low voice, where was Elinor.

"Is not she here?" said Laura, looking round; "I have been in the garden, but she refused to come. I think she said she was going to write a letter."

Leslie was obliged to content himself; and taking up a book, sat watching the door which, every time it opened drew his eager eyes, till the appearance of some uninteresting figure caused them to be impatiently cast down again. Laura's attention went nervously to the clock, which ticked on so composedly, and would not hasten towards half-past nine. Nor even when the half-hour had leisurely lifted up its voice twice, to denote that it was come, did the outer bell sound for prayers, till another full minute had gone by; and yet further, several seconds, which seemed like hours (as they do to a man under the surgeon's hands, or hanging on the edge of a precipice while relief is coming), passed by, before the butler threw open the door, and announced, after the manner of butlers, "Prayers is ready." Laura rose at once, and with a bland smile, walked alone out of the room followed by her brother, by Leslie, and by the few men who were guests in the house. Nothing could have answered better, for as they crossed the ante-room, which opened on the garden, Elinor came hastily in, the veil on her head, and Sir Peter following closely. Laura saw Leslie's start of displeased surprise; he went to her and offered his arm, regardless who observed him, or what they thought.

"Where have you been?" he said, in a very low voice.

"Miss Chanson took me into the garden and sent me on an errand."

Leslie had just heard that Miss Chanson bad been alone in the garden, and that Elinor had said she was going to her own room.

"But you are not alone," said Leslie.

"I could not help it," said Elinor; "he came out to smoke and met me."

"He always smokes in the garden at night. You knew it?"

"Indeed, indeed, I did not."

"Dear, dear Elinor, do not ...."

They had now crossed the hall and entered the parlour where the servants were assembled. The necessary outer decorum prevailed, but stormy was Leslie's bosom, sad and frightened was Elinor's, while holy words and pious attitudes alone appeared to the public ear and eye. Laura hastened Elinor away with her after prayers, saying that they must be punctual to-morrow at breakfast in order to be ready for an expedition which she had arranged, and however early it was they would now go to bed to prepare for it. Leslie was so much in love that he did not venture on being offended with Elinor; he no longer assumed an authoritative manner with her, that was too paternal, too like a guardian, but he had a grieved look and way towards her, wholly natural and unpremeditated, which brought the tears into her eyes. He saw them, and they atoned for everything.

"She is sorry," he said to himself; "she knows she has been wrong. No doubt it is his fault more than hers. Still, why did she use the worn out plea to Laura of writing letters. Why did she, to me, invent the pretext of being sent on a message. And she tells these little lies so innocently, she would deceive any man, if he were fool enough to think there is a woman in the world who does not lie." He stamped the unoffending boards of his room as he came to this conclusion, and walked up and down till he reflected there was such a thing as going to bed.

And now came Monday, the day on which the drawing, the needlework, the gardening, the professional duties, if there be any, or the gun and the dogs, the fishing rod and ride if there be none, are resumed after one day's suspension. There has been the village church changing the disposal of the morning and afternoon from the six days' course; there has been, perhaps, a different style of books read, an abstinence from some favourite employment, and, at all events, there has been the sight of the poor man's holiday; twenty-four hours, in short, in some way different from other similar periods, and a consequent mark left upon Time. Laura awaking, saw before her three wretched days, in which she had to fight against the natural order of things in order to bring about a base purpose of her own; a purpose liable in a high degree to failure, she was disinclined to get up and do this iniquitous battle, although it was not that the iniquity struck her, but her own hard fate in being unable to obtain the object necessary to her happiness without such a struggle.

"And why is it?" thus her thoughts came over her, but not worded; "why is it that I love him thus?—he is not eager to please me, as others are. I am obliged to cultivate conversation before it runs freely between us. He does not seek out my wishes as my poor brother does, and as William Mansfield and the other man did whom I could not bear. No! I must sacrifice plans and comforts to him. If he once loved me, if I once knew that he would be sorry to go away, then I could renounce him—perhaps—but if he went now, he would forget me to-morrow. I should think of him, and he would not think of me; he is so commanding among men, he cares so little what is thought of him; he is so acceptable in society, so beautiful—if I could but know I had power over him—shall another?—she ......?"

Laura sprang out of bed and took up her self-imposed burthen. How carefully were all the minute cares of her person attended to, and how mechanically; but as for her mind, its habits were not those which led her to be true with herself; hence all was slurred and burred within, and she had a most imperfect view of what she herself was doing. But at half-past nine she descended clean as a white pebble from a running brook, neat as a rose-bud still bound by its unfolding calyx; agreeable, attentive, handsome; but within, there was a heart constantly conscious in its way of beating that something was wrong; there was a dry mouth which disliked the business of talking, and hated that of eating; there was the sense of hearing strained to catch one voice, and rebelling because that voice was not addressed to her. There was fear over all, that some of the many words might be said which would reveal those secrets which lay so near the surface, and which any chance might lay bare from the covering she was able to draw over them.

Chance did not show itself favourable to-day; for her plan had been to keep the lovers apart by dividing the party between carriage and horseback, and to visit a show place in the neighbourhood, of which the possessors were friends of hers, and their society and chaperonage round their house and garden, would prevent the formation of tête-à-têtes. But before breakfast was over, the clouds let fall their long-threatening torrents, and in a very short time Mr. Chanson declared the expedition impossible.

"It will be too late, even if the rain stops by mid-day," said he; "you must do something else. Come, we'll have a game of billiards first, and then, when you two women have written a dozen letters, and worked your frills, or your kettle-holders, you shall help me to change the shells out of the library to the new cases. I want the labels neatly written, and little card boxes made. I am glad it rains."

"I will be glad too, for your sake," said Laura; "Elinor, will you help?"

"Oh, yes!" said Elinor.

"You can't want to write more letters!" said Laura, availing herself of the shot which accident opened to her.

"No," said Elinor.

"Have you finished all?" asked Leslie, in a low voice.

"I have not," said Elinor, in a voice still lower; "but say nothing. I shall be so glad to do Mr. Chanson a little service."

"His sister believed that you were employed in writing last night," said Leslie.

"How could she," said Elinor; "I went to bed by her desire as soon as we were upstairs."

"Equivocator!" thought Leslie.

Evening came, and with it a change in the weather. Before setting, the sun shone brightly out, and it left the autumnal garden in a gentle haze of warm air, where the smell of the fresh earth and the excited flowers, and the air renovated with moisture, flattered every sense of eye and ear.

"How delicious," said Laura, when she and Elinor stood again outside the window which opened on the walk; "let us take our bonnets and walk for ten minutes."

They did so, and at the end of that time, Laura said she must return to the house. "Elinor, will you be so good as to go as far as the clerk's, and ask him to look in our pew for my prayer book? the one in vellum, you know, which my brother gave me. I forgot to bring it away, and I want to gum down the label on the back before it gets rubbed off."

"I can't do that to-night," said Elinor.; "in the morning if you like."

"Why not?" said Laura, turning full round upon her.

"Sir Peter does not allow me to walk alone."

Laura burst into laughter. "What, must Sir Peter shut himself up every time it pleases you to take the air?"

"I don't mean that" said Elinor.

"Oh! you fancy he means to assassinate you, or take hold of your hand ...... or ......"

"No!"

"Or that his sole object in walking out is to share the delights of your conversation, and wait upon your presence. Upon my word his sole object is, rather, to smoke his pipe."

"Oh! yes."

"Which object he pursues in the garden and the fir-grove. Therefore, even though that frightful young man were to amuse his leisure with the sin of tobacco, you would be quite safe my dear in walking to the church. Now go, will you, Elinor?"

"No," said Elinor, "I cannot. Mr. Leslie does not choose I should."

"Oh! now it comes out. She's afraid of beiing scolded, is she? What! she has been scolded already, and has cried and said she would never do so no more, no! never. What a good child!"

Elinor stood with tears in her eyes. "Yes," she said, when Laura scornfully waited for an answer; "I said I never would do what he disliked."

"I never heard anything so babyish in my life. Why you are no more fit to be a married woman than an infant. If you let a man tyrannize over you in that way while he is your lover, he will be cruel as a husband, and sick to death of you in six months."

Elinor stood silent: her colour rose under the hard words and fearful prophecy, but she did not credit it, and yet would not contradict the utterer.

"Now, my dear child," said Miss Chanson, "for your own sake let me entreat you to behave a little more like a woman. Have a little independence, just enough to make him think you his equal. If he finds fault with things right and innocent, don't mind him, go your own way. Stand up to him. Men like to be stood up to."

"Very well," said Elinor, smiling, "I will remember what you say."

"And go to the church for me," said Laura, smiling also, "there's a good girl."

Elinor shook her head.

"You will not?"

"I cannot."

"Say will not at once, if you mean it. Well?"

"Indeed I cannot, I will not."

"That will do. Then will you be so very obliging as to go in and tell my brother, that I am obliged to go on an errand, because you will not, and that I ...... and that you ...... what you choose."

Laura turned her back, and set out hastily; but in a few seconds she stopped, and looked back, she had expected that the gentle girl would have run after her, but there was Elinor, standing quite still, watching her. Laura ran back—

"What! will you do neither one nor the other, do you defy me? am I to be defied in my own house? ridiculed? go to the church directly, or let me believe you are the most ungrateful of women."

"I will not walk alone this evening," said Elinor.

"Will you do this, then?" said Laura, commanding her voice to the lowest and calmest tone. "Will you pass this evening in your own room?"

"I am very sorry I have offended you," said Elinor, "I will do whatever you bid me," and she turned away, and went straight into the house, and upstairs, while Laura dashed the tears of passion from her eyes, and inveighed against the cruelty of the young girl, for triumphing in her victory over the lover of her benefactress.

When she reached the drawing-room it was still empty. She opened a book of drawings on the table, and composed her agitated frame. A few minutes brought in her brother and his guests, and then the first inquiry was for Miss Ladylift.

"She told me she was going to write letters," said Miss Chanson, demurely.

Sir Peter instantly glanced at his cousin, and smiled. Mr. Leslie caught the smile, and his eye turned in the same moment upon Laura, but she was looking straight forward, as innocent as a bird. He perceived, however, that young Bicester was swallowing a scalding cup of coffee, and that lounging apparently from one window to another, he silently opened the door, and disappeared. Leslie, with no attempt at mystery, went out directly after. The evening was growing very dusky, but he saw the man he deemed his rival, entering the avenue, and hastily followed him. Sir Peter was alone; and that he was alone, surprised Sir Peter. But that the person who joined him should be Leslie, thoroughly annoyed him, and Leslie on his part was equally angry at finding the young soldier thus apparently awaiting a page: rendezvous. The one overtook the other, and they walked together a few yards in silence.

"Are you going into the park?" said Sir Peter, at last.

"No; are you?"

"No." Again there was silence; then Sir Peter began again.

"I never knew you choose this walk before."

"Did not you?"

"No."

Sir Peter shook the ashes from his cigar bitterly, and then turned suddenly, and walked in the opposite direction. Leslie, who seldom smoked, took out a cigar, in order to give himself some reason for being here, and puffing with undue vigour, excited a great smoke, and marched to the end of the avenue; here he turned, and about mid-way, the two young men met, and crossed each other, each sending out a large gale of tobacco, and looking as happy as he could. How long this was to go on, Leslie did not like to conjecture but at all events he did not intend to leave the ground while his rival occupied it, even though they should walk thus till morning. Sir Peter it seemed was not so persevering, for before they came across each other a third time, he stepped on one side of the path, and left the avenue by a wicket which led by a back way to the house. Leslie immediately stood still and flung his cigar as far as its weight would carry it, and then collected his thoughts with more form than the presence of Sir Peter had allowed.

"It is too plain, that he expected her," he said to himself; "then he has already met her. Yet I warned her—besought her—but he is a villain, availing himself of her untaught, guileless, nature—inexperienced, bewildered, humble as she is! If he knew my claim upon her, she would be safe. Yet impossible! shall the silly coxcomb know that it is my promised wife, whom he has hoped would come at midnight to meet him? Impossible! He is going, thank heaven! to the other side of the world ...... tempest, fever, sword, and shot, pursue him!"

Thus he stormed within, standing beside one of the stern fir-stems, which threw a steadfast shadow on the turf from its branches between the moonlight and the ground. Nearly half an hour passed, in which time Sir Peter felt fully persuaded that his rival must have been tired of his suspicion, and have left the avenue. He himself had been to the saloon, where still the fair Elinor was not, and with some hope, rekindled from the malicious eyes of Laura, he returned again to try his fortune. Slowly he paced down the avenue, and failed to perceive the dark figure beneath the fir-tree. As he came on, it advanced suddenly from the shadow. Sir Peter started slightly.

"I forgot something," said he.

"Did you," said Leslie.

"Yes!" said Sir Peter, and again they passed each other, and Sir Peter proceeding to the end of the avenue, opened the gate, and went finally out. "What right has he to act dragon?" said the young man, as he returned home.

Next morning, Tuesday, Leslie and Miss Chanson were walking together through the garden to the conservatory. Elinor looking from her window saw them, and was pleased that her angry guardianess should be in company with one who she felt would speak even better of her than she deserved. So warbling some low notes with her melodious throat, she turned away to put in order part of her simple wardrobe, with skilful fingers well versed in the arts of hemming and darning.

"She told me," said Leslie, to Miss Chanson, "that you sent her to her room last night."

Laura started, not knowing how much of their interview had been repeated, and looked Leslie inquiringly in the face.

"If I did ......" she began, and paused.

"Tell me one thing," said Leslie, "did you do so from any idea that it was better not to leave her walking alone?"

"Why do you ask me?" said Laura, quite at ease again; "what does it matter?"

"No, no, it does not matter ...... very much," said Leslie; "only is it possible, do you think that she intended to join ...... that is ...... to meet ......"

"Only that could have justified me," said Laura, candidly. Leslie was silent. "I told you long ago," said Laura, at last, "that I hoped your confidence was not misplaced."

"No, no, it is not," said Leslie, "but she has been in an unnatural atmosphere. She came here full of innocent mistakes, and we undeceived her too hastily; she has lost the landmark for all minor proprieties."

"Then I wonder," said Laura, "that she should think it necessary to conceal them, by such complicated statements."

Leslie again was silent. "She is bewildered," said Leslie, at last, "by the admiration she excites; I have not flattering words so freely at command as others, and perhaps, she is better amused by those who have them, than by me."

"That's quite impossible," said Laura, very quickly; then as if frightened at what she herself had said, she added hastily, "perhaps she wants character, she is like most women ......"

"Oh no!" said Leslie, sighing, "she has a firm purpose, hidden under her soft exterior. I will talk to your brother the moment we are alone, on Thursday, and I will make her mine before any other candidate dare come between my treasure and me."

It was now Laura who was silent. To hear a purpose announced which directly contradicts the secret object of one's endeavours and desires, is like a blow struck right upon the heart. Why cannot the blinded eye of our companion see and choose the path which we perceive so plainly is the one fit for him?

Leslie was out of spirits, and when he had gone through the flowers of the conservatory mechanically with Laura and the gardener, he walked back with her, till they came in sight of the house again, and then turned into the park, and wandered away alone, whither he did not care.

Laura proposed twenty things in order to entangle Elinor with her cousin, but was baffled in all. Elinor would not take a lesson in billiards, would not learn to sit the pony, would not teach Sir Peter a duet, would not lend him a book of her own—she declined all, even before they were fully proposed; and at last, upon the arrival of some morning visitors, attached herself to the mother of the party, who did not choose to walk far, and never left her side the rest of the morning.

Laura did not venture upon any scheme for the evening, but she saw with bitter pleasure, that Leslie, by seeming accident sat by another than Elinor at dinner, and that when they were all assembled in the drawing-room, he and Elinor seemed to want subjects of conversation, and were grave and embarrassed in place of that joyful glee which Leslie's face had so often assumed, to Laura's anguish, when listening to, and talking with Elinor.

Wednesday was come, and now Laura had her last blow to strike, the one that must undo her if it did not succeed. There was a feeling in the house about seeing the last of Sir Peter, since after to-day, he could be seen and heard no more. He was not to go shooting alone, nor to take a solitary gallop; he was to walk with Laura and the rest, he was to visit the stables with Mr. Chanson. Even if those who were not to be travellers had something better to do, there would be time for that to-morrow, when there would be no more time available for Sir Peter. Mr. Chanson, Leslie, and Sir Peter, were all to set out early on the morrow. They were to drive together to the neighbouring town, and there to separate, the two first to pursue their way to Mr. Chanson's property, and the young soldier to go on to London where his final preparations would be made. Leslie, in a doubtful state of mind, was looking out for offence and cause of unhappiness; Elinor, in an humble one, was unconsciously giving it. She was accustomed to the discipline of a conventual school education, and had learned a degree of patience, which made her take Leslie's absence as an unavoidable trouble, of which she must not complain. He also had been accustomed to the natural teaching of school, but had acquired a different lesson, for his spirit had been one of those which make others yield to them, and had gratified every wish as it arose. Her meekness, therefore, in resigning him for a certain number of days seemed indifference in his eyes, mystified as he was by Laura; and though he loved her the more anxiously for her coldness, he imagined that it gave him greater reason to suspect that another occupied part of his place in her heart. Elinor felt there was something wrong, though she knew not what, and Leslie was conscious of a restraint, unlike those happy days—the few days—when he and she wandered among the fields and woods.

"So now it is come to the last evening," said Sir Peter, as he and Laura sat together an hour before dinner, in her own apartment. "I have had a very pleasant visit, and I shall not forget it."

"And what remembrances do you carry away from our nun?" said Laura.

"Oh! hang the little nun, I am tired of her; I can make nothing of her, and really I believe our meetings have all been either my own doing, or accident. She cares for nobody but Leslie."

"She does not care for him," said Laura; "he is half offended, that she should take his departure so quietly."

"Did he tell you so?"

"No—not in so many words—but words are not always necessary to explain meanings."

"You are so clever, Laura! you see everything."

"Women have that faculty, you know. Now, I would venture to lay a wager, that if this last day, you were to write, soliciting one last interview, the interview would be granted, or you would get a kind excuse for not granting it."

"Oh! it is too much trouble."

"Where is the trouble? there is pen and ink, and I will tell you what to write."

"But it is hardly fair."

"Fair indeed! as if any measures were to be kept with her. What has she done by me?"

"You! oh, I can't keep in my head that you can possibly have any regard for a person who does not adore you."

"No, it is most unworthy," said Laura. "I will do better ...... there, there ...... shake him off—forget him. But that little girl I should like to unmask, nevertheless; come play out the play, write her a little love-letter."

Laura now took her portfolio on her knees, drew the little writing table close, and laughing and coquetting, composed a note which amused Sir Peter, and which he copied at Laura's side, and promised to remit to Elinor. Laura agreed that he should do so, but just as he was leaving the room, recalled him, and told him to trust it to her care, for that she could manage it much better than he. Sir Peter tossed her the note, which she caught in a very pretty attitude, and kissed the tips of her fingers to him as he paused at the door, to give her a last look.

It was ten o'clock that night when a woman wrapped over her head and whole figure in a cloak, brushed by Sir Peter, as he walked in the avenue, and as she passed thrust a note into his hand. He caught the hand that gave it, but it told nothing except that it was enveloped in a glove. Rather than be detained by him, the hand slipped out of the glove, and the figure darted into the thick shade, and disappeared. The glove was merely a concealment for the hand, for it had plainly been held loosely, as a measure prepared beforehand to avoid detention; but it was a woman's glove, of delicate size, and was finished with a plaited ribbon, such as Elinor frequently employed herself in fashioning. Sir Peter laughed as he recognised it, and placing it in his bosom, proceeded by the light of the moon to decipher, though with great difficulty, these words—

"I cannot come to-night, Mr. Leslie forbids me to go out.—ELINOR LADYLIFT."

Poor Elinor's ill-starred billet!

CHAPTER X

See that man walking up and down his room all night, except when at times he flung himself on the sofa, burying his head in his clenched hands. The little shred of paper lay sometimes on the table, sometimes on the floor, trampled on, crumpled, torn; again spread out, and read with unabating fury. Beside it lay the glove, which together with the note had been brought to him by Laura, and which with scarce any words she pressed upon him as the tokens of Elinor's falsity. He saw them and believed; they seemed to him to indicate that the meetings between Elinor and the young soldier, which he had persuaded himself were the effects of accident, or of mere momentary thoughtlessness, were parts of a long-continued understanding between them, and that to Elinor they had become so habitual as to make an apology necessary, when she was unable to keep the appointment. How could Leslie doubt? there was her handwriting, there was the glove of her fine hand—false hand, false heart!—her he had trusted then in vain! the innocence by which he had remodelled his own intentions, did not exist. Laura had stabbed him with this poisoned dagger, and left it to work out her own ends; and frantic indeed was the effect of the wound she had inflicted.

As soon as day dawned, Leslie left the house, and continued his agitated walk up and down the garden where he knew, by many a morning's experience, it was Elinor's practise to walk before the breakfast hour, and where of late he had usually joined her.

The cold October air chilled his frame, the heavy rime, almost frost, weighed down the remaining flowers and the dripping grass; the sun, long hidden after it had left the horizon, struggled with the mist that filled the whole atmosphere. It was late before the day became as light as the hour warranted; and the savage impatience of Leslie grew almost to delirium.

At last, a window which opened to the ground from one of the sitting-rooms was heard to rise, he stood still, partly hidden by the trunk of a cedar, and saw shrouded in a gray cloak, and a hood concealing her face, Elinor step into the garden, and move along the walk to his place. He instantly came forward, and silently seizing her arm, saying no word, answering no look, dragged her forward with a hand which she felt violently trembling, nor stopped till they were in the wood together, deeply hidden, as the words they had to say together required hiding. Then letting go her arm from one hand, and opening the other, he showed her the little note and the glove, which it had clenched as they came along.

"Your's?" he said, fixing his bloodshot eyes on her face.

"Oh, it is my glove which I had lost," said Elinor, holding out her hand for it, and looking up at Leslie, perplexed, whether to smile or yield to terror.

"And where, and how did you lose it?" said Leslie; "tell me, explain ...... confess that ......"

"How can I tell?" said Elinor, frightened, and with a trembling voice.

"No; in one sense you cannot tell, shame forbids—your false nature forbids—can you tell me this? Did that glove deliver that note? look at it."

Elinor looked at the little paper in his fierce hand, and recognised the first words of the billet she had written months before.

"Leslie," she said, "I do not know, how should I? it is so long ago."

"Silence!" cried Leslie, "you can deceive me no longer; no affected innocence, no well-continued deceit can perplex or blind me now. This is then your writing?"

"Yes," said Elinor, earnestly looking in his face, and saying the one true word, for she had nothing else her nature permitted her to say. Then his fury burst out—

"Devil! angel! woman!" cried he. "You have failed then to deceive me! you confess—we are even again. I was on the point of believing in virtue—you fail—I am free, falsest, hardest, perfidious woman ......"

Elinor interrupted him. "What harm have I done? did not you tell me I might write to you."

"To me! oh, well-acted innocence! yes, I was so cunning. I thought to have surpassed you in cunning; would I had ...... any crime better than to have been smiled at till I was a fool, and for an instant to have been held in your mocking snares—but it is over—seek your other victim, if you will, follow your soldier if he will have you! I have my eyes open at last."

"As I live and stand here, Leslie, there is no human being who cares for me, or whom I care for, but you."

"Words! sweetest words!" cried Leslie, "falser than sweet, and crueller than false, were I not free. But they are nothing to me now; no, nor those; tears, nor those clasped hands, nor that well-acted fear—no, no, no."

"Leslie!" cried Elinor, laying her hand upon his arm.

He caught hold of her hand, and crushed it in his, like one whose nerves have escaped control, and are contracting upon the object that excites them with mechanical fury; then his hold relaxing, he flung her hand away, and uttering a groan, which at the same time he struggled to repress, lie turned, and rushed from her sight.

Elinor was changed to stone, by all that the few minutes just passed contained; she gazed on the blank space where Leslie had been, and had said such killing words; she thought of herself, entering the garden but now, about, as she believed, to converse with her lover, and part from him for a few days, soon never to part again; and could by no means realise that his love had turned to fury, that he had said he was about to leave her for ever. Her mind and body seemed paralyzed, and when at last she recovered strength of both, enough to move from the place where she was, she did but return with benumbed steps to her own room, and there sinking upon the floor, lay crushed and bowed together, sobbing as though her comfortless heart must break.

The guilty cause of all this woe, once more glittering in outside show, like some splendid serpent, was descending in apparent peace to the morning meal; but her bosom also burned with anxiety, and she trembled internally at the thought of what aspects she might meet. Might she not there see, perhaps, Leslie and Elinor, with all explained between them, and united for ever against her. Might she not see Leslie frowning and despising her, Elinor sheltered by him against all future malice, or should she see them alienated from each other, and she herself successful. She opened the breakfast-room door, with a hesitation unseen on her serene face, and glanced round; but her conjectures were all wrong, for although all else were assembled, the two were not there. Again her heart bounded with fear, that they might be together, too angry to keep up any appearance of good will with her; and after enduring the doubt and anxiety for a few decent minutes, she affected to be anxious what could have become of Elinor, and left the room to look for her.

When she beheld the young girl, she knew that her artifices had succeeded, and triumph filled her heart. Elinor, abandoned by what was all the world to her, and terrified at her own solitude, no sooner saw a familiar face, than she rose and flung herself on Laura's shoulder, straining her in her embrace with inarticulate mourning. Laura thought of her own fine lace and muslin, which Elinor was deranging; and raising her, so as to stand free of the sorrowing girl, asked her, with a voice as kindly as she could make it, the cause of her distress.

Elinor's explanation would hardly have made anything clear, had not Laura possessed already a more perfect knowledge of the circumstances than she could receive. The single point she cared about was, what had become of Leslie, and Elinor could only repeat that he had flung her off, and rushed away through the thick wood, where she soon had lost that last sight of him.

"Last indeed!" said Laura; "after such a parting, there can be no reconciliation. What have you done Elinor?"

"Indeed, indeed, I have done nothing! he is too cruel to me."

"Yes, too cruel; he has been very hard on you; he should have overlooked what faults your ignorance of the world led you into. Think of him no more, give him up as he has given you."

"I must die before I do that!" said Elinor.

"Nay, nay, dear child; dying is not the thing in question. Here, dear, take a little water ...... can't you? well, lie down, or sit down, I will come again to you—but they are all waiting now—I will bring you a cup of tea."

And Laura departed, going down stairs elastically, and filled with the image of her rival, whom she had left behind humiliated, robbed of her beauty by tears, and abandoned by the man who once abandoned Laura for her. She made the excuse of headache, and having over-walked herself, about Elinor, and now if Leslie had but come in, would have been perfectly happy; but his absence raised new fears in her heart, that in giving up one, he would not renew his allegiance to the other, nay, might commit some rash act, her fear and her love began to dread what.

Breakfast was nearly over when a note was brought to her brother at the other end of the table; he opened and read it to himself, and Laura all the time was obliged to keep smiling at her cousin, who sat beside her, for his last breakfast in her society, but whose words at this time conveyed no meaning to her at all.

"What have you got there, Lawrence?" she said, at last; "you look perplexed?"

"This fellow Leslie," said he; "he writes me word that a messenger came for him from home, and he is obliged to set off at a moment's warning. Who saw any messenger?"

"No, sir," said the servant, who was waiting at breakfast.

"Who saw Mr. Leslie go?" said Mr. Chanson.

"It was not I, sir."

"Go to his room. Are his things gone?"

Nothing was gone.

"Nor does he say anything about sending them," said Mr. Chanson; "he'll write again, I suppose—but what a nuisance for me. Now I shall have to go alone ..... I shall stay, I think."

"Oh! no," said Laura; "go, and perhaps he will meet you. What can have happened. Perhaps his house is burned down?"

"Perhaps he is arrested for debt?" said another.

"Perhaps the bank he deals with is stopped?" said a third; but both Mr. Chanson and Sir Peter looked at Laura, suspecting a quarrel between her and Leslie. She neither said nor looked any answer, but she was officious and obliging in promoting the arrangements of the party, and when she fancied her brother still hesitated about his journey in consequence of Leslie's secession, she exerted herself to persuade her cousin to accompany him, and demonstrated that with a little extra, exertion he might both perform this friendly office by Mr. Chanson, and also get through his business in London before the time came for the sailing of the ship. Sir Peter, for her sake, at last consented. Mr. Chanson was satisfied to exchange Leslie for him, and all seemed arranged to the general satisfaction. But five minutes before the time of departure, Laura, watching her opportunity, followed her brother into his study, where he was giving his last directions to a servant, and sending the man from the room, suddenly put her arms round her brother's neck and appeared to be stifling the sobs which stopped her utterance.

"My dear child—Laura—sister—what is it? Speak to me—can I help you? Only tell me who has grieved you."

"Has he not forsaken me, Lawrence? Shall I ever see him again?"

"Who is gone, Leslie! is that it? I was afraid something had gone wrong between you."

"Oh! I have been so wrong; I have acted so foolishly. Only that little girl's artful manœuvres bewildered me. This very morning she appointed to meet him in the garden, and I could not bear it. I ...... I ......"

"You quarrelled with him, did you? and is it that which keeps Elinor up stairs and drives Leslie away? But what right had you to quarrel with him; tell me, had you any?"

"What right!" said Laura impetuously, "except that of a betrothed woman?"

"Is it so?" said her brother seriously; "in that case I have no business to go looking after prospective votes. My business is to stay at home, and see that my sister has justice done her."

But Laura sank almost on her knees, her arms clasping her brother all the time.

"Oh! no, Lawrence—no!—don't ruin me quite. Any interferences of that sort would destroy my happiness for ever. He loves me—he will return to me, but it must be by his free will. Could I deign to accept a hand that did not bring a heart ...... but the heart is there—it is mine—my own fault has alienated it for an instant, but if it be left to itself it will not fail to return. If he departs at my rash word, my penitent word can recall him."

"I thought you implied it was he who had left you?"

"I cannot measure exactly what I say. I am distracted. I came to tell you all."

"Let me remain with you, Laura; it will be best."

"No, no! I would not have him think you know anything that has passed between us. Go, dear Lawrence, I will recall you if it prove necessary. All I want is to have nothing concealed from you on my own part, and to be able to trust my brother through good fortune and evil."

Real tears came into Laura's eyes, as though she had been spectatrix of the same scene at a play. Mr. Chanson was moved, and repeatedly pressed upon her his offers of assistance. She, however, continued steadily to refuse, and returning with him to the hall, suffered Sir Peter to think she had been reddening her eyes with sisterly weeping for him, and at last saw them all depart, and was very glad when the house was finally cleared, and she was at liberty to put the finishing stroke to her plans.

CHAPTER XI

Leslie's anger and despair carried him to the end of three days, and when those were elapsed, the mild image of Elinor began to break through his stormy passions like present moonlight in a sky thick with black clouds. His own harshness, exercised upon so delicate a feature, shocked himself; her fear, her courage when she laid her soft hand upon him, her utter bereavement when he left her in the deep wood alone, wounded his heart. He believed in all the faults which he had believed at that moment, but he began to think they were immeasurably punished by him; he felt himself the greater sufferer under that punishment, and when his spirit revolted from the idea of receiving again the broken vows which she had once made him, he yet felt impelled to implore her pardon for the manner in which he had resented her perfidy.

When he had persuaded himself that such was the object which made him long to see her again, he at once gave way to his desire to do so, and a very short time saw him again in the neighbourhood of Chanson Wood, haunting every spot where he could hope to meet with Elinor. But it was all in vain, the cold weather caused all the shutters to be closed with declining daylight, so that he had no such chance as the summer had afforded him of investigating the dwellers of the rooms. No old favourite haunt was visited by her footstep, no morning or evening hour brought her out to behold its beauty.

Leslie wandered about for four and twenty hours, and then made his way to the house itself, and inquired for Mr. Chanson. He was not yet come home.

"Miss Chanson?" She was walking in the flower-garden. He had not words to ask for Elinor, but followed the servant silently into the garden, dreading more than wishing that the two ladies might be together. But no; Laura only was there. While the servant was within hearing, Leslie's tone and manner preserved their common-place, but they were no sooner alone than he broke out eagerly,

"Can I see Miss Ladylift?" Laura hesitated. "What! she cannot forgive me?"

"Could you forgive her?"

"A man has always a right to forgive a woman. Where is she?"

"Mr. Leslie ...... don't you know?"

"My God!" cried Leslie; "I have killed her!" and his wild eyes searched and commanded Laura's face for the fearful words he expected.

"Not so," said Laura; "but she is not here. Before I could communicate with my brother, before I could reflect what to do, she insisted on setting out for her convent."

"Her convent?"

"After you were all gone, and I returned to her room, she had already made her preparations, and no efforts of mine could detain her. I did what I could; I sent to Mr. Roundel, you know him, my brother's man of business, and requested him to take charge of her on her journey, which he did."

"Tell me," said Leslie, laying hold of Miss Chanson's arm, and speaking in a very low voice; "was she willing that he should go with her?"

"Why?" said Laura.

"Was there not another whom she expected to join her."

Laura's colour rose to scarlet in-her face.

"It never occurred to me till now," she said; and in truth, Leslie had suggested an event in the plot which Laura had overlooked in contriving it.

"Where is the companion you gave her?" cried Leslie.

"He returns to-morrow; but surely if what you fear had occurred, I should have heard it from him."

"I can't tell," said Leslie, as if unable to argue, able only to fear and suffer. "I shall see him the moment he comes home. Farewell! Ours has been a troubled intercourse, Miss Chanson," he said, offering his hand; "forgive me much that you have against me, and which you will forget when I no longer darken your happy home." So saying, he turned away and walked up the garden, Laura pursuing him with stedfast eyes.

"Does he think to leave me thus?" she said to herself; "is all over between us, does he suppose? and he goes without a look behind, unconscious that there is a spell upon him, and of necessity he must return." Then as she saw him ascend the steps of the terrace, her eye could not but mark that he did so with a step very unlike the decided strong movement of his general pace. "He is ill," she said to herself; "I may lose him even in trying to win him. Better even that, than that he should belong to another."

The day was by this time dark, and Laura, whose general habits were luxurious, and who was to be found on cold evenings in her lounging-chair at the side of a bright fire, her feet upon the warm hearth, abundance of wax light on her marqueterie table, her book, her work, her dress all in keeping, on this night muffled her person in a gray cloak, and going herself to the stables, at the time of the hall supper, when she knew one lad only would be left there, caused this boy to prepare her pony carriage with uncompromising haste, and, with him to drive her, set off in cold and darkness for Cantleton, the town where Mr. Roundel lived. She had readily answered Leslie that he would return to-morrow, her instinct being on all occasions to gain time; but she was perfectly aware herself, that he had already been back a whole day, having in fact received from him the assurance that he had conducted Elinor to the convent whither all Laura's skill and power had been exerted to make her fly. She had, however, felt in a moment that she must see him before Leslie could do so, and had gained twenty-four hours by her ready lie.

It was ten o'clock before she reached the town; she had a humiliating part to play, that she felt, but at least she would do it in a grand, unquestionable way, and would come out of the house quite beyond being assailed in person by any remarks which might be made by its indwellers when she should be gone. Besides, she had brought a sum of money, so considerable (under the name of paying Mr. Roundel's expenses on his journey) that the acceptance of it—and she was quite sure it would be accepted—would constitute an acknowledgment that further services must be rendered in return. Still, while she waited for him in his parlour, where the fire was out, and the chairs all set back against the wall, she had uneasy beatings at her heart which kept her standing; and which she thought to subdue when he came in, by taking a seat with as much dignity as if she were in her usual position of command. She did not begin with any reference to the strange lateness of the visit, for the cause of it would soon, she knew, seem stranger than the visit itself, but without apology or explanation opened her business.

"You have done me a service, Mr. Roundel," Laura began, "in conveying that young lady back to France."

"Since it was for your interest, as I understand," began Mr. Roundel.

"For her own, I beg it to be understood," said Laura.

"Oh! certainly, certainly."

"Did she seem delighted at returning to the convent?"

"I can hardly say delighted," answered Mr. Roundel.

"Indeed! I am surprised at that. What could then make her wish so much to return? Did anybody come to welcome her?"

"A maid-servant answered the bell when ......"

"No; before you reached the convent? In fact, Mr. Roundel, I have cause to suspect that her eagerness for the journey—for the trouble of which, by the by, allow me to offer you this note"—Mr. Roundel looked at it, and began to understand that his answers must take some shape which he did not as yet perceive—"her eagerness must be connected with the departure of ...... you knew my cousin, Sir Peter?"

Mr. Roundel bowed assent.

"You must be aware that her fancy for this gentleman could never be encouraged by us; but it is possible that infatuation on his part ......"

"Very possible," said Mr. Roundel.

"What, you had reason to suspect?"

"Nay, I cannot deny I had my suspicion," said Mr. Roundel, thinking that expression would suit whatever came next.

"Indeed! and what followed?"

"What followed?" said Mr. Roundel. "Well, to tell the truth, nothing very particular."

"You trifle, sir; if that young man gave you cause to suspect intentions which she favoured, I conclude that you were unable to conduct your charge safely to the convent."

"I assure you," answered Mr. Roundel, hastily, "I safely delivered Miss Ladylift into the hands of the Superior; what might happen afterwards, I cannot say."

"Unfortunately, Mr. Roundel, I fear that I can."

"Is it possible?" said Mr. Roundel. "At all events, I discharged my duty."

"Undoubtedly, there is no fault of yours; but however distressing to myself to speak upon such a subject, I feel it my painful task to mention to you, that should any one inquire about her from you, you had better put an end at once to any interest taken in her, by stating that, on too good authority, you know her to be unworthy of it."

"Upon my soul!" said Mr. Roundel; "and if particulars are asked, I can refer ......"

"It is not probable that I should enter upon such subjects," said Laura, in the most dignified manner; "I have already said, perhaps, too much; and when I came to you, I did so as to a friend, who, I trusted, would relieve me from the necessity of saying more."

Mr. Roundel bowed, and Laura, rising, prepared to depart.

"But if I am asked where I left the young lady," said he, "what must I say?"

"The truth, sir," said Laura, very loftily. "What you yourself know to have been true as to her arrival, and what you understand from me to have been true with respect to her subsequent departure."

"I understand," said Mr. Roundel, in a very low voice. Laura's eyes met his; then, in a grand way, she requested his pardon for disturbing him at this late hour, and bidding him good-night, sailed out of the house, Mr. Roundel following her to the pony carriage, and when she was gone shrugging his shoulders, and muttering an epithet I will not repeat.

The next morning, Leslie, who had passed the night in walking about a bedroom of the inn in the town, wandered forth, dragging through the time till he might inquire when Mr. Rounder's return was likely to take place.

"Master was already at home," the maid answered, and Leslie and he soon stood face to face. Mr. Roundel had thought over the matter, and had resolved in his own mind that the rich and powerful Miss Chanson was the injured person in this, to him, obscure history, and that, on the whole, in adopting her views of it, he should best consult his own interests, as well as her wishes. He therefore scrupled not to give Leslie the version Laura had taught him.

Leslie received the story so calmly, and so much as a matter-of-fact, that Mr. Roundel became almost persuaded that he himself had been telling the truth.

"A very fine young man," said he to himself, when, after thanking and wishing him good morning, Leslie disappeared down the street. "A fine man, and takes the result of his adventures quietly;" and with that Mr. Roundel turned back to his office.

Leslie meantime reached the inn, and wished to inquire what public conveyance would first start on the road to his own place; but the words which he found himself using were not those which bore the meaning he wished to convey. He tried to frame the name of the town nearest to his own house, and spoke as slowly as he could in order to fasten the sound and the idea together; but even then he failed, and perceiving that he had done so, he turned away by a great exertion, and forced his limbs to carry him a few step's; then a great dizziness came over everything, and stumbling forward upon a seat which he just descried, he there lost consciousness of himself and everything else.

He was known at the inn as the guest of Mr. Chanson, and when the doctor had seen him, and declared him dangerously ill with brain fever, and when it became apparent how desirable the presence of some responsible person might become, the landlord sent information to Chanson Wood of what had happened. Mr. Chanson had returned the evening before, and his hospitable nature led him at once to the desire of receiving his sick friend, and to have him nursed under his own roof. Laura seconded him, and looked upon all as the favourable working of her fate, which was relieving her own brain from the necessity of forming further devices for the achievement of her scheme.

A carriage fitted up for bearing an invalid, was despatched with a handy footman. Mr. Chanson went on horseback to the inn, and before the end of the day, the unconscious Leslie was conveyed to Chanson Wood; and lay there helpless, like one entangled of old in the meshes of a corrupt and beautiful enchantress.

The struggle between life and death was more severe and more solemn than Laura had anticipated. It lasted very long, and sometimes forced upon her the real probability of that which she had hitherto put to herself in words only, namely, that Leslie would die. "If he should die?" she said to herself, believing it, and trembling at what it implied, but she threw off the image, for it was in disagreement with all, the web she had been weaving, and whatever unfavourable report was brought her, attributed its worst gloom to mistake or ignorance, which falsely represented the real state of things.

But it was very long before the demon of the fever could be cast out of Leslie's frame, and when at last it was expelled, it left him shattered, exhausted, and so utterly devoid of the strong sense of life he had hitherto enjoyed, that it seemed to him impossible ever to be again the free, careless, powerful being he was accustomed to be; rather, he felt that he had only escaped the death of fever to go down more slowly, and as surely, into the grave, where all things are dark and at rest. His mind had begun under the auspices of the pure love with which Elinor had at last inspired him, to have healthier feelings than were habitual to it, of happiness and of virtue; but the disappointment of his newly-born faith and hope had swept away all the better feelings which grew up with them, and a more gloomy scepticism as to whatever was just and good never darkened any human bosom than that with which he got up from his long illness.

It was now five months since he had fallen down unconscious in the inn at Cantleton, and been conveyed by Mr. Chanson to his own house. He had just become able to walk about, and his only desire was to go home and die there. He felt the burthen of his obligations to Mr. Chanson and Laura, and heartily wished they had left him to perish when he fell ill, and have neither tormented him with a second long process of dying, nor with a debt to them, which nothing he could do was able to pay. He made efforts beyond his present strength in order to get away the sooner, and the re-action when he was alone piled over his spirit the mountain weight of its oppression.

Laura watched him; and it seemed to her the moment was coming when she might finish her enchantment, and prove whether the spell had been woven strong enough or not. She did not deceive herself as to the fact that he loved her not; he was obliged, but not grateful; he was waiting impatiently to leave her, though there was no one whose society he would seek in exchange. She could not talk so as to interest him now; though he did his best to renew the easy gossip of bygone days. Still she had strong hold on him, and knew it. She had kept the secret of his engagement to Elinor inviolable; and he was thankful that it had never reached Mr. Chanson. She had falsely insinuated to him that her own name had been coupled with his through the county, and that the result was injurious to her hitherto sacred reputation; he had believed her; and though he said to himself the fault was hers, and so must be the penalty, yet it was difficult to feel himself in no degree committed; and, finally, his fixed expectation of death and his disenchantment with all faith in happiness, persuaded her that he would be indifferent to one scheme of life almost as much as to another.

It was one early April day that she proposed to him to walk for ten minutes in the garden; and he, eager to prove himself strong and independent again, complied. Laura knew how weak was his frame, and wondered that he could force himself to pass and repass so often up and down the dry gravel walk; at last, she proposed to rest under a bower which kept off the active breeze of April and the bright sunbeam, and Leslie consenting, they sate down side by side.

"This short walk is long for me," said Leslie, "but my ability to perform it reminds me that I am able at last to relieve you of a burthen which you have so kindly supported. To-morrow I will find my way home."

"If you have resolved upon a thing," said Laura, "you will do it; remonstrance is useless."

"Yes," said Leslie; "but it is a kindness in you to speed me thus."

"The kindness of letting you free yourself from my society without useless contradiction? you cannot say yes to that; social forms forbid you; but honesty forbids you to say no."

"Not so much honesty," said Leslie, "as the conviction that I am a dying man. I cannot fence with words at this time; I have strength for nothing but the bare truth, and I allow that to die in a dark corner at home, is what remains of my ambition."

"Alas!" said Laura, "since you say those cruel words, I know that you mean them; I too have a meaning," she went on.

"Nay, do not tell me," said Leslie, for he felt she had a scene in store, and he shrank from the trouble of it. "There is no meaning, no purpose which has anything to do with me, or in which I have a part to bear."

"I mean," said Laura, suddenly, "that in your death, more die than you."

"By no means. I was a pleasant fellow enough last year, but this one, I am a mere curtain, a drop-scene; when I am pulled away, all the stage will be bright again."

"And all this for the sake of one who is unworthy to be remembered!" ejaculated Laura.

"One," said Leslie, shuddering, "whose name must not be a sound again, for God's sake. Unspoken as it is, it galvanizes life back to my heart."

"Forgive me, Leslie, I am grieved to have said it."

"Forgive!" he answered, " there is much of that needed on all sides—not by you, however. These are idle words."

"No, not idle," said Laura, "I am not without need of forgiveness, though others want it more."

"Don't say so, for you do not mean it, nor have I wit or strength to unravel your feigned humility. In my best days I always was idle about contradicting those who spoke ill of themselves."

"You are hard," said Laura, "and oblige me to look very narrowly to my judgment of myself. Perhaps you are right; though I may have done a wrong thing, still it is possible that, like Othello, I was not the most guilty."

"'More sinned against, than sinning,'" said Leslie; "I told you so."

Laura paused, she thought he would ask in what she had been sinned against, but he said nothing, and she was obliged herself to make use of the opportunity she had opened. After a minute's silence, therefore she resumed.

"Society makes crimes out of things which are innocent by Nature. When man is in prosperity a woman is obliged to deny that his good or evil destiny can interest her, but when fortune has forsaken him, when he is unhappy, ill, lonely, is it unwomanly then to say she feels for him?"

"Alas!" said Leslie, "I am not deserving of one kind feeling. I tell you truly that I cannot rouse one in return, for any human creature. Who could, when his grave was dug, his shroud making?"

"Do not talk thus, Leslie; even were it true, a woman, were she friend, sister, wife, would know no comfort, except to watch and support every step which remained of his earthly career to one in such trouble."

"I am no judge of that," said Leslie, smiling; "I think, however for my own part, that I am like an unsociable lion, who stalks into the wilderness to die, and leaves the lionesses to enjoy themselves in the world again, when he is gone."

"The world," said Laura, forcing back conversation to a grave tone, "looks to you for its opinion of me."

"Nay," said Leslie, "it cannot be so unjust."

"Cannot be!" cried Laura; "why use that vain phrase when nothing is more certain than that it is? But heed it not. It is fair, I know that the woman who has ventured to feel unasked should learn to the uttermost how she has offended the pride of man."

"On the contrary," said Leslie, "our manly phrase is that we are much flattered by such generosity."

"And your meaning is that, you despise it."

"That depends upon whether it gives pleasure. For my part," he went on, "she whom I loved is dead, she is as if dead, and that deadness has spread over me, so that I am already a mere citizen of that quiet country, from returning to which I have been unblessed with a short respite. Let us talk no more."

"Yes, I must say what I have to say; I am wrong to do so, but your desolate words wring it from me. I liked you prosperous, I love you miserable; answer what you will, these are plain words—I cannot deceive."

"Oh no! I can never be deceived again, I can never feel again. I tell you truly, those words of yours leave me unmoved, therefore unsay them. I can easily forget."

"No, Leslie, they are as true as that they have been spoken."

"They have a meaning, certainly," said Leslie, "but hardly that which they bear at first sight. Let us understand each other: do you believe that busy bodies would respect you more if you bore my name? A dying man's name is not much to give."

"Leslie, can you think, that even if the world has been so unjust, (and so it may have been), such selfish thoughts can prompt me in what I say?"

"Call them by some other title than selfish thoughts, and they seem a fair motive enough. Only be honest with yourself; confess to yourself that you are moved by some such motive, and that you know I am so indifferent to the whole world that I cannot love nor esteem any member of it; nay, that kind words, such as you have used, pain or annoy me, more than any amount of indifference."

"You hate me for them," said Laura.

"No, I cannot hate, I cannot love; it is to me as if you said my name could be useful to you, and as if I hesitated whether to give it or not. Can you still wish it?"

"Can I do otherwise?" said Laura.

"Yet reflect: should you not buy too dear the suppression of certain rumours which you say exist, if to attain that end, you must undertake to walk by a dying man to his grave?"

"Leslie, you know me, or affect to know me very little. I have said the word which once you almost said to me, I have truly said it; you knew long since, that you were dear to me—you forget it—it was indifferent to you. It was not I who forgot it, and now, when all forsake you, I say again, I love you."

"Remember, even those words leave my heart unmoved. Laura forgive me, but I seem to myself like the statue of stone, upon taking whose hand we have all seen such unpleasant consequences ensue at the opera."

"Can you jest?" said Laura.

"No, I will not—I will calculate. I hear those strange words of yours comparing them with scenes which I confess remain in my memory. I reflect on the evil you say the world has cast on you. I repeat that I feel nothing, and that what I do, or what I forbear is indifferent to me. And after that—if you will—be my wife."

Laura held out her hand, he took it; not as a friend takes his friend's, not as a lover grasps that of his mistress; but he laid his palm upon the back of her hand, and rising, led her silently towards the house.

Pale, unanimated, uncongenial, these two went slowly along the walk, while the clouds of a suddenly overcast spring sky veiled the light of the day. It was like Adam and Eve wandering through the world after they were cast out of Paradise.

Next day Leslie told Mr. Chanson of his engagement with Laura, and departed to his own house. All approach to tenderness on the part of Laura, he treated as if it aid not exist, and Mr. Chanson, a matter-of-fact man, was completely puzzled. But Laura was contented. The project which had seemed almost impossible was executed; and when she pondered over the situation in which she found herself, she shut her eyes upon the fact that Leslie's misery was her own creation, and dwelt upon that of attaching herself to an unhappy and suffering man, till she believed that she was both generous and unselfish in so doing.

Leslie meantime reached the Tower in a state of perfect exhaustion, and he thought with pleasure that the next tidings Laura would receive of her bridegroom, would be in the formal style, and on the formal deep-edged paper of the undertaker. He sank into a stupified sleep, at the length of which the few servants in his house were too uninterested in their master to wonder, and probably did him the best service in their power by neglect. He woke and wondered that he did so, and now without rule and without physic, proceeded to live or die, just as day by day might determine. His time was passed in the most absolute solitude, so that through the twenty-four hours he would sometimes not find occasion to utter a word; he would lie at length on an easy chair, his gloomy eyes fixed on one spot, or wander into the air, and out of sight, nobody knew whether afar off, or just hidden by the first great tree, or projecting buttress of the old wall; and here suffering his ideas to come or go as they would, the gloom of his mind seemed to settle thicker and thicker, as weary day was added to weary day. To himself he appeared drifting into that dark chaos, which, as he believed surrounded on all sides the brief light of conscious being; and the impression was the stronger, because he had lost entirely the activity of those mental faculties which had hitherto been his pride and pleasure. He never read, never composed, never remembered the images with which former reading had stored his mind. Nature was uninteresting. There was sound without music; forms, but no beauty; actions, but no crime, and no virtue. Even the bitter past was not enough to account for his total shipwreck; he was convinced as fully as if it had been matter-of-fact, that the near approach of dissolution it was which thus covered him over with shadow.

In this mental condition, he wrote several times to Laura, to break off the engagement she had taken on herself. To him it was a matter of indifference, but to her it would plainly be mere misery. Laura, however, heeded no more what he said about himself than she had heeded the evil reports of the physician, when he was ill at Chanson Wood. She had her own intemperate hallucination about Leslie, which had begun in fancy, went on in jealousy, and was confirmed by the measures into which she had thrown her conscience, and her very soul, to secure him. It was not likely that she should stop now. If a thing could be done twice, it would very seldom be done the second time. But the girl who marries for money must reach the enjoyment of coaches, respect, and fine clothes before—if it were to be done again—she would not do it; the man who sets his fancy on power, must have possessed the pride of governing, and the homage of the multitude, before he can tell whether the sacrifices made for it were worth while. In the same way, Laura, with a mind incapable of self-control or self-sacrifice, acknowledged no alternative except being the wife of Leslie; and thus, under gloomy auspices, their marriage was privately celebrated in the drawing-room of Chanson Wood, during the month of November of this year.

CHAPTER XII

Leslie's excuse to himself for marrying as he did, was the ever present conviction that he must die. But for that sick state of mind he could have done no such thing. He believed the world to be closed upon him, and circumstances drifting him towards Laura, he had wearily yielded himself to them for the few months he expected to know the last of life, and its society.

Time, however, as any one more accustomed to illness would have anticipated, produced a gradual amelioration; and it was with reluctance that Leslie found himself compelled to acknowledge a renewal of the life which his will was ever prompt to lay down. The commonplace matters of a household in which he was called to act, did him good. A detected poacher, for instance, a cheating tradesman, a groom who neglected a horse; and he would have been ashamed to suffer the intellectual despair which consumed him, to show itself among practical men, or domestics of his house. He had letters to write about ordering claret, or paying for a dog-cart, and not deigning to ask assistance, performed these commonplace tasks, and found they made inroads on the army of his phantoms. When he mounted his horse again, the familiar exercise was useful to him, and the first animal he rode being excessively perverse and obstinate, he had no time to meditate by brook sides, or through shadowy lanes.

Thus through the winter he went on resuming his intellectual health, though the moral sank to a lower and lower tone, as he continually reflected on the dream of innocence and virtue which had existed only to make him the dupe of a girl of seventeen. That false girl was ever present to his ideas, he repented his forbearance, he imaged her to himself in the society she had chosen, he analysed over and over the apparent guilelessness, the exquisite innocence of her demeanour, baffled how to reconcile them with what he knew of her treason.

"But did not I myself bid her follow her soldier, if he would have her?" he repeated to himself. "Heaven! how infinitely far was I from believing such a coarse word could resemble the truth."

He had more thoroughly believed that he was speaking the truth, when he told Laura, that in marrying her, she was perfectly indifferent to him. So she was indeed, and very soon did Laura, after reaching the point she had allowed to dazzle her, begin the descent which led away from that glittering height. All her life she had so far taken pleasure in being popular, as to make people as comfortable as she readily could; her brother's habits and fancies, her cousin's whims and wishes, she had never traversed, nay, much more had promoted, and this same patronising and good-humoured compliance she was now quite willing to extend to her husband. But in return she had hitherto got gratitude and worship, and had been exalted to the place of oracle in all matters which admitted a reference. There was a difference now; for she had become the companion of a man excessively her superior, whose time and habits were spent on objects which required rather her exclusion than her assistance. She attempted changes, but found quickly that the ways of the house must be the ways of the master; and that there was an unbending will in this respect which stopped her at once. To gain the upper hand, she tried jealousy, she tried sickness, she tried magnanimity, but all in vain; Leslie kept her to her bargain, that in marrying him, it was her whim and fancy which were gratified.

"Poor Laura" he said to himself, "I promised her I would die, and here she is suffering all the penalties of believing me. I am sure I intended it."

Laura's good humour soon gave way to these trials; her next effort was anger, passion, reproach; but to those he put an authoritative stop. Love was far from them both he knew; but ridicule should be equally far; an outer decorum should prevail in his house; and as for the rest, were not women proved to him to be creatures undeserving respect, incapable of goodness?

Rather more than a twelvemonth had passed since their ill-omened marriage; and however apparent the unsuitableness of Laura's character became, the secret of her machinations remained undiscovered. In the early days of her marriage, the apprehension that some chance might reveal it, had continually haunted her. Every letter which she saw Leslie reading made her anxious; she watched his face for the sudden lighting of discovery; she dreaded when he put it by and said nothing about the contents, that suspicion had been excited which he would silently follow out; she examined his letters before they reached him, if she found it possible to do so; and made pretexts, which afforded mirth to the servants' hall, to look at the addresses of those which he left for the post; every acquaintance awakened her fears, lest some chance word should reveal the real position of those whom she had represented under such false colours; and in her anxiety and alarm, she had invented many ingenious excuses for avoiding communication with all who could by any chance be acquainted with the persons and circumstances of the past months.

But as time went by and no revelation took place, as Leslie remained unaltered, and no kind of allusion to the past ever arose between them, the silence in which all was involved began to give her confidence, and that which might have happened at any moment, and which did not happen, seemed like a thing gone into oblivion, which never could possess a tangible shape again.

Laura grew bold in impunity, and then followed the reflection that she had secured the position she now occupied beyond the power even of discovery to dispossess her. By degrees she began to feel as if the very discovery would have its advantages. There would be at least a momentary triumph, in showing how she had outwitted Leslie; and when his superiority weighed upon her, unsoftened by any kindness on his part, there would arise a longing on her's, to show that she had once baffled his talents, and possessed herself of a place from which no efforts of his could now remove her. It was a heavy secret, which she dreaded to betray, yet found it difficult to keep, and which would come almost into the shape of words occasionally, yet shrink back in terror when there arose a real chance that it should escape.

In this uneasy state, irritation arose out of many a trivial circumstance; harsh words were said on her side; cold scorn of them was implied on his; he forgot them, and was neither more nor less annoyed by the companion who had forced herself upon him than he had expected to be; his interests were all apart from her, and were tinctured by the gloomy atmosphere which still clouded his spirits. The habits of his mind made him resort as necessarily to reading, as his bodily appetite to food; but the only subjects which could fix his attention were the stern expression of great passion, the details of strong purpose and of grand crimes—whatever was bitter towards man, whatever lowered human nature, he dwelt upon, and thence broke away to his own gloomy reflections, pursuing the phantom of past faith and hope to their disappearance, and racking himself against the problem of Elinor's character and conduct (as they appeared to him), which it baffled him to explain. He wearied himself with restless exercise, and sought the reality or the semblance of danger as a means of forgetting for a while his vain longing for the past; and his hatred of the present. Miserable, but resolutely silent, he lived through the days.

In these circumstances Mr. Chanson found them, when, in the end of the autumn following their marriage, he returned from a moor belonging to him in Scotland, and came to pay a visit at the Tower. He saw nothing that was going wrong; outer forms were carefully observed, and he was satisfied with the smooth surface which was presented to his eye; the bitter words which Laura could not restrain, were unanswered by her husband, or made to pass for jests; the complaints she suggested were unreasonable; and her brother, who, in the midst of all his admiration, had sometimes felt her government rather a severe one, secretly applauded the manner in which Leslie reigned so absolutely, yet without any ostentation of dominion. He was well pleased with his reception, with the amusements of the wild and extended country, and finding himself alone with his sister and his brother-in-law, his talk flowed more freely than it did when tramelled by society.

They were all three one afternoon upon the terrace of the Tower, where the building wanted most repair, and where Leslie had arranged some plans of alteration.

Laura was very much opposed to these; she had always drawn the elevation of her brother's cottages, and had as constantly met with unbounded applause; and when she first heard of the necessity of building at the Tower, she had prepared a drawing of battlements and loopholes, which Leslie negatived at once. The subject had been ever since a sore one, and Leslie avoided it as much as possible. To-day he had been far from willing to make this spot the scene of their saunter, but Laura, who was in a bad temper, knew no ease till she had got her brother there, and could vent her discontent.

"I should not wish this picturesque building spoiled," said Laura; "should you, Lawrence?"

"No, who would?"

"We don't agree about the way of restoring it," said Leslie.

"No; I incline for preserving the character of the building. I don't see any reason for destroying a beautiful thing, merely because another person wishes to preserve it."

"Look here, Lawrence," said his host; "this fragment of a wall fell when I was a boy, climbing the Tower. It and I came down together."

"And you not killed?" said the Squire.

"So it seems," said Leslie.

"Is that the reason," asked Laura; "why you mean to leave the Tower with a great rent in it?"

"But I don't mean to do so."

"Nay, the other day when I showed you my idea of the restoration, I understood you to say it did not suit you to do anything to the Tower."

"Pardon me, I did not feel the merit of your suggestion; but I was and am aware, that restoration of some kind is essential."

"When do you mean to begin building," said Mr. Chanson.

"I have not thought much about it," said Leslie.

"Then you may leave it to me. I have thought, and I have a right to do as I please with a part, at least, of the expenditure of the house."

"What is your meaning?" said Leslie.

"Once I could do as I pleased with all that was then my own."

"That's a strange observation," said Leslie; "let us speak of it this once, because your brother is here. Lawrence, I beg of you to say whether the implied reproach is well founded."

"Laura, my dear, really I am obliged to acknowledge that for once you are wrong. Leslie's magnificence to you ...... do recollect!"

"Wrong? did you ever say such a word as that to me, while I was so happy in your house."

"One more word," said Leslie; "be just with yourself. In bringing you here, did I deceive you?"

"Oh, dear no! I am not so easily blinded as others are who boast very much of their penetration."

"What are you saying or meaning," said her brother, who observed Leslie's heightened colour at this last thrust, and the sudden compression of his stern lips. In fact, he understood Laura to allude to his fatal secret with regard to Elinor, which she had hitherto kept from her brother, but which he would prefer at once revealing, to having it held out as a threat whenever she might lose her temper.

"It is quite true," said he to Mr. Chanson, "that I was strangely deceived by one to whom your sister alludes."

"No, no, Leslie!" cried Laura; "I did not mean that."

"What do you mean? What does anybody mean?" said Mr. Chanson.

"It is best to cast away secrets," said Leslie; "who could bear one clinging about him like a poisoned shirt? That young girl ......"

"What! Elinor?" said Mr. Chanson; "nay, Laura told me all about her the very day we parted, when Peter took the place with me which you threw up, and went I know not where ...... but what does it matter? Laura forgave you."

"Forgave me?" said Leslie.

"Well, whatever word lovers please to use. You were reconciled at all events, for here you are man and wife."

"Do choose some other topic for discussion," said Laura; "I will explain what he means presently," she added, in a low voice to Leslie.

"No, allow me to understand your brother," said Leslie; "I remember the day perfectly, but being absent, you know, I was not aware of the movements of the rest of the party. Your nephew took my place?"

"He did. Laura persuaded him."

"Yes," said Laura; "they travelled part of their journey together. Now, Lawrence, you promised to walk to the brook. Let us go, or it will be too late."

"Well, if you wish it," said her brother; but Leslie interposed.

"Did you ever learn where Sir Peter went when you parted?"

"To Ceylon, man! We all know that.."

"But in the interval between the time when you parted from him and he set out, are you aware where he went?"

"Nowhere at all," answered Mr. Chanson, "except where I went. I never did part with him till he went abroad. How could he go anywhere?"

"I heard a very different tale," said Laura.

"That's unaccountable," said Mr. Chanson; "why, you know very well that I went to sea with him for a dozen miles, and came back in Mendip's yacht."

"Are you sure," said Leslie to Laura in the commonplace tone of conversation; "that you did hear a different account?"

"Did not you?" said Laura, in an abrupt, scornful voice.

"Yes. I was told another."

"And believed it," whispered Laura, under her breath.

Leslie looked at her fixedly. Mr. Chanson went on speaking. "Peter was sorry enough that his visit was at an end. He was a great admirer of Laura, and in a lesser degree of Elinor also. It was a pity she could not marry him."

"Do you speak so easily of what passed?" said Leslie.

"Why not? if she had liked him it would have been all very well."

"She had no mind to marry so poor a man," said Laura.

"Poor little thing! Any fate would have been better than shutting herself up in the nunnery," said Mr. Chanson; "I often think of her."

"She is there?" said Leslie, in a voice of perfect composure, and Laura could not but start at the self-command which enabled him to catch at the revelation her brother was unconsciously making without betraying that it was new to him.

"Certainly; it was entirely her own choice to go there, was not it, Laura?"

"Her own, solely, I suppose we must conclude," said Laura.

"You hear of her sometimes?" asked Leslie.

"Yes; every three months an ecclesiastic connected with the establishment acknowledges my remittance of her little income. It is little, indeed, but since she has chosen that life, they tell me it is better not to add to it."

"You have never failed to hear from him?" asked Leslie.

"No, except when I was absent from home. Laura had the letter then. Did not she mention it?"

"Not I," said Laura; "was it worth while? I am tired of the subject—I am cold. I shall go in ......" and she departed, walking leisurely towards the house.

"I see how it is," said Mr. Chanson; "Laura has not quite forgotten the fit of jealousy which Elinor caused her, but take no notice of it. Women are naturally unreasonable, and must be allowed for."

"In what have I given her cause?" said Leslie.

"Oh! I am alluding to the time before your marriage, to your great quarrel, when we all parted."

"She complained to you?"

"No, no! don't think it; but seeing her so unhappy, I could not but inquire the cause, and then, for the first time I learned your engagement, and her fears that Elinor had entangled you, though in love all the time herself with young Bicester."

"All that, she told you?"

"Yes."

"Indeed!" said Leslie; "never mind. I begin to understand. And Sir Peter, what did he say?"

"I never said much to him on the subject. But in what little he did, say, he alleged in his own excuse that having learned your engagement to Laura, from Laura herself, he thought himself entitled to make love to Elinor, as you had no right to do so—all the time acknowledging that she avoided him as much as she could, and that he was wrong to have so persecuted her."

"Did he say that?" asked Leslie; then, as Mr. Chanson made no answer beyond a brief "Ay," he repeated in a tone which would have startled one more observant than the Squire: "Did he say that?"

"Yes: honourable of him was it not? I should have been quite deceived in that young girl had not Laura told me beforehand of her little skittish ways."

Leslie kept silence, but with a sudden effort he broke in two the short stick which he held in his hand; his brother-in-law looked at him in astonishment.

"By Jove! that's a strong arm. Is it some trick? How do you do it?"

"Sometimes one has a wish to do a strong thing," said Leslie, pitching away the broken pieces.

Mr. Chanson rose from the stone wall where he had been sitting. Leslie also moved, and took the way towards the house, whither, following the impulse thus given, the Squire also bent his steps, and entering it by the first door they came to, Mr. Chanson turned into the hall, and Leslie, the moment he was alone, strode up stairs in quest of Laura.

She knew he was coming, but did not know herself what mood his coming would excite in her. She was frightened at one moment, angry and fierce at another; sometimes he seemed the Leslie upon whom she had let her fancy doat, and then the Leslie whom at other times she hated with all the violence of her former love. He found her, at apparent ease, in a lounging chair, with a newspaper in her hand. She looked at him as he entered almost as a wild animal would look, excited to self-defence, and ready for flight or fight as the movements of the intruder might determine. Leslie came forward to the table which was on one side of her, and there he stood, saying at once in a perfectly calm voice,

"I am come to demand account from you of the deceit you have practised upon me."

"Have I deceived you?" said Laura; "did you believe me?"

"Yes; a lie like yours there is no defence against. Unsay it."

"What am I to say and unsay?"

"Where is that young girl?"

"Whom do you mean?" said Laura.

"Elinor Ladylift."

Laura laughed. "You speak out. Elinor Ladylift is in the convent of St. Cécile. You heard my brother say so."

"Did she at once go there, stay there? did no one ever seek her there? did she take refuge and remain there?"

"So Lawrence said."

"You dare not trifle!" said Leslie, striking the table with his hand, and advancing a step nearer to Laura. "Do you know it of your own knowledge?"

"I know nothing to the contrary," said Laura.

"You acknowledge, then, that your representations were false ...."

"False!" said Laura.

"Go on. There was a letter brought to me by yourself. Explain it."

"I have often brought you letters," said Laura.

"There was a letter purporting to be written by Elinor Ladylift to your cousin Bicester. Was that letter a forgery?"

"It was her writing," said Laura.

"What is behind in your meaning? Dare you say she sent it to him? Dare you ....."

"I did dare, and it answered my purpose," said Laura; "you believed. I could have laughed at times to think how the great, manly intellect yielded to despised woman."

"Laugh! yes," said Leslie; "that is the very word for perfidy and crime which in due time have lost their covering, and are carrying you to the ruin you have wrought for others."

Laura sprang up. "Nay, not so; guilty I have been, but what has made me so? Miserable I may be, but I ventured all for that which I have won—I am yours!—you are mine! In that hope I knew nothing, cared for nothing, except itself. Whatever I have done, you, you Leslie should pardon me, for that for which I perilled my very soul was your love!"

But Leslie drew back as she approached him. "Love!" he said; "is it by that name you call a vile fancy which was contented patiently to destroy life and hope in its object? How nearly you have dragged me to death, how far from happiness. But no more of that. The past has been yours, the present is mine. I care nothing for unravelling the web of your perfidy. Enough that I know all you have said and done is false. Enough. I have borne with you while what you acted passed for true. Now do you bear with whatsoever befalls you, dragged on your own head by your own deed! I have done."

He left the room at once. Laura sprang up before he was gone, and called him, but he closed the door and went to his room. Here, like a man who once possessing the amulet that ensured the blessing of his life, and who, dropping it into some profound lake, stands despairingly gazing into the waters; did Leslie stand awhile, horror-stricken at the knowledge of his own fate. All that he had left behind he now saw and knew; all the clouds that had hidden past actions rolled away, and left the view of the sunny land behind him, which he had exchanged for the dreary pestilential region now surrounding him. The horror of his entanglement bewildered him; the thought of all those days and months, wherein reparation for his cruel injustice had been delayed, pressed upon his senses; the choking feeling of distance and alienation wrought so fiercely on him, that of all impossible things the most impossible to his imperious and self-indulged nature was to delay by even another hour to seek, nay, to force an interview with Elinor, leaving the issue of that interview to be what it will.

Springing out of the first torpor, he took measures at once to leave the Tower. He provided himself with what money was in the house; he thrust his papers and letters into the drawers, and summoning a servant, bade him instantly prepare what was necessary for a journey, and bring it after him to the neighbouring town, whither he himself would proceed at once on foot. To put himself into action was the only relief he could find, and hastily he passed through the hall, and out on his road away, able he knew to conceal his emotion from any one he might casually meet, but not trusting himself either with inaction or with the sight of the woman who had ruined him.

When joined by his servant, he took charge himself of the portmanteau, sending back the man without message or explanation, and hastened alone with all possible despatch to the coast. Here he took the first conveyance which crossed the sea, and was put ashore at early dawn on the Breton coast, at a village but a few miles from St. Cécile's nunnery.

It was Thursday, and he remembered having heard Elinor say that Thursday was the day on which the pensioners were chiefly permitted to receive their visitors. He therefore pressed forward with all haste to add one more chance to those shadowy chances which remained of ever beholding that dear face again, but his heart died within him to think how faint they were; sixteen months' grief, neglect, Time, what had they done? Was she even there? Was she perhaps lying at perpetual rest beneath a reviving turf? or if she lived, was she by this time a professed nun, alive, but dead to him? Could she forgive him? had he not believed accusations which the deceiver herself had thought it incredible to impose upon him? Oh! what mountain piles of sin had he not committed against the gentlest, most charitable, most defenceless of beings! He saw the little low building rising before him with emotion that almost choked his breath. It stood on a common which descended to the sea-shore, terminating in rushes and sand hills; a marshy pool or two glittered in the sun, and some small cows were picking up the coarse herbage under the care of a boy and girl bareheaded and barefooted. The building itself was low, and formed a square, of which the side opposite Leslie was unpierced by windows, and except for one low door at the upper end, it might have been, what Leslie's gloomy feelings likened it to, a tomb.

At this door he knocked, and presented a letter he had prepared, entreating permission, in her guardian's name, to speak to Miss Ladylift. The lay sister took it, and returning before long, conducted him to another part of the low, gray square, where she admitted him to the parlour and there left him. There was already a young girl, laughing with a motherly woman, and with a child, who seemed the girl's sister. Leslie turned to the window, his back to these people, his face therefore not to be seen at once, although he could watch whoever came in at the door. And before any long time, there was the voice he loved so fearfully.

"Qui me demande?" and Elinor stood there looking at the group within.

"One not worthy so much as to ask pardon," said Leslie, turning to her and approaching.

"Mr. Leslie!" cried Elinor, starting as if a bullet had struck her heart.

"That's the last word you said when I last beheld you," said Leslie; "if I was mad then—if there was a curse upon me, can you forgive me?"

"I forgave you long since," said Elinor.

"That is, you would wish me no harm," said Leslie; "but is that all—is forgiveness only that?"

"Yes, only that" said Elinor; "but indeed, full and free forgiveness, for though you were more unjust than I understood, you know that, now, or you would not be here. Good-bye."

"No! no! no!" said Leslie, taking her hand, and drawing her to the window, while he spoke very low. "It is not all so lost between us. You are to me all that woman can be to man. You have my destiny in your hand; you must hear me."

"There is nothing to hear," said Elinor; "you renounced me, and I found shelter here. Your wife sent me."

"I have none," said Leslie.

"How! I know from herself that you have married Miss Chanson."

"No; there is a fiend who lays claim to me; a serpent stole round me, but I am free!"

"You speak madly," said Elinor; "I will go. May you be happy! Farewell!"

"Is that all? you loved me once, Elinor."

"I try to forget all the past," said Elinor. "It is quite gone... Let me go now."

"You try? Do you say that? Alas! is it your will never to see me again?"

She did but bow her head as if in assent, but he felt her trembling hand.

"Oh, my beautiful! my perfect!" he cried, grasping that hand and trying to look into her eyes; "you love me still! that love is still there. You are too true and good to say 'No!' when you cannot but say to yourself 'It is Yes!'" Elinor hid her face as far as she could on her own shoulder, the tears ran down her cheeks. "You loved me once," he repeated.

"You tried to make me," said Elinor.

"Oh, angel! I did. It was long before your heart gave way; very long before your colour mounted when I came, but it did at last, and you never can forget it."

A sob broke from Elinor.

"La pauvre enfant," said the old mother, who was present; "laissons les!"

"Mais, ma mère, c'est si joli," whispered the young pensioner.

"Fi, donc, Jacqueline! un jour cela t'arrivera à toi, peutêtre. Faut être compatissant," and the good woman drew away her girls, leaving the room to Leslie and Elinor.

Leslie drew a chair for her, and sank down before her. "I have been so miserable," he said, dropping his face on her knees, "I am so—not at this moment, with your precious hand in mine, but if I loose it and am again what I was before I grasped it, I cannot go on living, I must die."

"It would be best if we both could die," said Elinor, "for on earth we must part for ever."

"Then you, you—are you happy?"

"No!" said Elinor, hiding her face and weeping.

"Alas! and once we were so near it—a word or two was all that was between it and us. I had it in my hand, I let it go. But it is near again, now we are near."

"How could you doubt me?" said Elinor; "I learned you thought I could possibly feel regard for one who was not you."

"Was I not mad? was I not a fallen spirit, into whose hands an angelic one had been put? But you are here again to save me; it is your destiny to save me."

"Do not talk idly; you have chosen your companion; your wife ......"

"Wife, hush! hush! there is one whom my heart acknowledges—here, this is my lawful wife. That woman is a mere adultress."

"You frighten me, Leslie."

"Ah! save me from what frightens myself—come with me now. Rise, fly with me. The world is waiting for us outside that open door. We cannot stay in prison; home, paradise, innocence, wait for us there! Come, my own Elinor!"

Elinor's eyes raised to his face, reminded him of that day, now two years old, when they before so innocently looked at him, wondering at his meaning.

"Could I leave my Mother so? Would she allow it?"

"No, no; but to be happy is our nature. I am good if I am happy, but make me miserable, Elinor, and what crimes lie before me!"

"Nay," said Elinor, "we need not be happy, but we must be good."

"Are not those two things one," said Leslie; "if it lie in your power to render a human creature the most blessed being on the earth, would you not do wrong to leave him in his misery? Must not that be wrong?"

"I cannot tell," said Elinor; "we must wait—one day, no doubt, we shall be happy."

"And will our youth wait for us, will our life wait?"

"Oh no!" said Elinor, "and I wish, with all my heart I wish, that we were old, and sick, and infirm, for then we should be near the land where I may come to you."

"Ah Elinor! but should those lands be dreams! Hear me! ......"

"I cannot, dear Leslie—oh yes! indeed you are dear Leslie—I only know we are parted for ever." Elinor forcibly rose, while Leslie with her hand in his, detained her, pleading, still more by the agony he suffered than by his words; and at that moment the door opened, and a tall handsome woman, her face bounded by the straight lines of her head-gear, came in, and Elinor at once broke away, and took up her place, pressed close against the Reverend Mother. She whispered a word or two to the young girl, and Elinor instantly stood freely up, and though the tears ran over, spoke out, "God bless you, Leslie! Farewell!" and vanished through the door, from his sight.

"You have brought her bad news, I fear," said the Superior.

"Yes, bad news," repeated Leslie, mechanically.

"Poor child! she has need of good. Ever since she came back here so suddenly, she has had a weight at her heart. What sort of people were they, those guardians of hers?"

"I know scarcely anything about them," said Leslie.

"Yet you came from them to her, I understood."

"Yes," said Leslie, "I am acquainted with them, but they are people perfectly indifferent to me."

"Do you think anything happened there to make her unhappy? Who visited chiefly at the house?"

"I knew one, a mere fool," said Leslie, "he thought himself clever, and was the gull of every female and male idiot that chose to deceive him."

"Then he it could not be, whom she regrets."

"Does she regret some one?"

"I cannot tell; her confessor knows; if she have proved the vanity of worldly worldy affections, I hope it may turn her soul to the holy bridal of the church."

"God forbid!" cried Leslie.

"And why, sir? Do you think she has no vocation?"

"Vocation!" repeated Leslie, hardly knowing what he said.

"Before she went to England, I thought so too," said the lady, "but experience of the world's emptiness and sorrow, often work a change for the better in the heart."

"Alas!" said Leslie.

"There would be a difficulty, of which you are perhaps aware," said the Superior.

"Difficulty? yes, no doubt—what is it?"

"When we have devoted ourselves to our profession, and have no leisure for the works which earn a living, we must have means of subsistence, live as hardly as we will. Therefore those who enter here for a life of devotion must be able to support themselves and others, by contributing to the general stock, or else they must come as menials, which would not do for her ...... but Elinor is so very poor."

"Is she poor?" said Leslie, with infinite pity in his voice.

"She has perhaps ten thousand francs for all her fortune; what you call, she tells me, sixteen pounds a-year."

"Oh! my Elinor!" groaned Leslie.

"With that she boards, and though it is too little, we keep the precious child among us, and she nurses, teaches, works, up to her best strength to make up what is wanted."

"Madam," said Leslie, "your society is most worthy, most deserving, would not a few thousand francs, bestowed on it in her name, secure her more comforts, more ease?"

"Such a donation might enable her to assume the veil," said the Superior.

Leslie shrank as if his hand had found itself on the bag of a nest of hornets.

"Don't let her do that, Reverend Mother," said he; "what is so dangerous as to encourage vows which are not voluntary, or of which the vower may repent? You might have a sin to answer for."

"Fear not," said the Superior, with dignity, "that we need the advice of a stranger in guiding our flock."

"No, no, I am aware of that—yet I entreat you forbid her to become a nun."

"Leave her to us, young man," said the Superior.

"I must see her again," said Leslie.

"Nay, your interview has already been long."

"And write to her."

"Give me your letter, if you wish to write, she shall have it."

"But if she wishes it, I may return."

"If she does not wish it, you cannot."

"And you will influence her. Oh! madam, there are miseries in the world, so great that you would pity the very devils whom you hate, for suffering them."

"There is a refuge from all," the Superior began—but Leslie broke away.

"I can't hear it now; preach to ease, not to the rack. Let me go," and he rushed away in a state of mind almost beyond his own control.

For several days he wandered round the Convent, asking admittance, and still refused, offering rewards to get a letter conveyed to Elinor, but denied; haunted by her tearful eyes, by her poverty, by her desolation. He was terrified at the possibility of the vows she might contract, and was for ever grasping at those blessings which might have been his and hers, but which were now mere shadows of those real things floating away, further and further into the past. He was fast bound in the meshes, which a woman, a mere woman, had found the means to twine around him, and fiercely did he resent the injury, and gaze sternly at her falsehood and successful deceit. It was in vain he raged against his bonds, which Elinor refused to assist him in evading, and which the hand that fastened them, even if willing, had no power to untie, though it had sought and forced the fatal spell to make them fast. She was his fate; a contemptible, but all powerful agent; a hateful presence which had forced itself upon him, and which held him imprisoned in sight of the felicity he had once grasped, and let go at the false accents of that despicable deceiver.

Violent were the passions of the strong but fettered man, fierce the hatred of the powerful but baffled intellect; wild was the fury of the man, who believed in but one world of good, and saw the mortal moments passing away, unenjoyed, and irretrievable.

Out of those hours arose a purpose. The reader sees the man, and knows the deed. From the premises laid before him, he need not indeed have concluded that even that man would do that deed; but since it was told, in 1855, that the husband killed the wife, so now, in 1860, it is explained why he killed her.

Carolyn Clive – A Concise Bibliography

IX Poems (1840) The second edition (1841) includes nine additional poems.
I Watched the Heavens: A Poem (1842) (The first canto of an unfinished poem)

The Queen's Ball: A Poem (1847)
The Valley of the Rea: A Poem (1851)
The Morlas: A Poem (1853)
Paul Ferroll: A Tale (1855) (The fourth edition contains a concluding chapter, bringing the story down to the death of Paul Ferroll.)
Poems. Including a New Edition of "IX Poems" (1856)
Year after Year (1858)
Why Paul Ferroll Killed His Wife (1860)
John Greswold (In two volumes) (1864)
Poems (1872)

Contributions to Periodicals

Poems
The Nursling — 1857 Jan 24th, in The National Magazine Vol 1.
The Chained Eagle — 1857 Jun 6th, in The National Magazine Vol 2.
The First Morning of 1860 — 1860 Jan, in The Cornhill Magazine Vol 1.
Beaten to Death — 1860 Jun, in The Constitutional Press Vol 3.
Christmas 1860 — 1860 Dec 29th, in Hereford Times
Seasons — 1861, in The Victoria Regia.
The Irish All Souls' Night — 1861 Apr, in The St. James's Magazine Vol 1.
November — 1865, in The Golden calendar: With a Perpetual Almanac

Tales
Rough Material — 1841 Feb, in The Metropolitan Magazine Vol 30.
The Great Drought — 1844 Oct, in Blackwood's Edinburgh Magazine Vol 56.
John Pike Yapp. A Tale of Mayo — 1857 Mar 14th, 21st, in The National Magazine Vol 1.
The Tower of Hawkstone Castle — 1857 Aug 22th, 29th, in The National Magazine Vol 2.
A Christmas Vagary — 1858 Jan 23rd, 30th, in The National Magazine Vol 3
Genuine Transactions with Principy Jack — 1858 Dec, in The National Magazine Vol 5
War—A Tale — 1860 Feb, Mar, in The Constitutional Press Vol 2
"Nadrione Spetnione:" Wishes Fulfilled. A Tale. — 1861 Apr, May, in The St. James's Magazine Vol 1 — 1861 Aug, Sep, in The St. James's Magazine Vol.2,
From an Old Gentleman's Diary — 1865 Aug, in Fraser's Magazine Vol 2
The Wishes Shop — 1865 Nov, in Fraser's Magazine Vol 72.
Ebb and Flow — 1867 Nov, in The Churchman's Companion Ser 2 Vol 2.

Play
A Minute Ago. — 1860 May, Jun, in The Constitutional Press Vol 3

Articles
Vanity and Self-Esteem — 1847 Jun, in The New Monthly Belle Assemblee Vol 26
The Swimming School for Women at Paris — 1859 Nov 12th, in Once a Week Vol 1

www.ingramcontent.com/pod-product-compliance
Lightning Source LLC
Chambersburg PA
CBHW021929170626
46807CB00007B/3039